21 SUGAR STREET

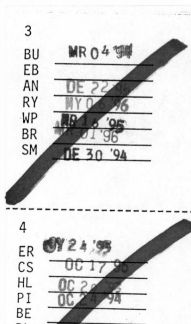

ALSO BY LYNN LAUBER

White Girls

LYNN LAUBER

21 SUGAR STREET

W.W. NORTON & COMPANY
NEW YORK ▪ LONDON

The text of this book is composed in Bembo
with the display set in Futura Book
Composition by PennSet, Inc.
Manufacturing by Courier Companies
Book design by Michael Chesworth

Library of Congress Cataloging-in-Publication Data
Lauber, Lynn.
21 Sugar Street / Lynn Lauber.
p.   cm.
I. Title.   II. Title: Twenty-one Sugar Street.
PS3562.A784A614   1993
813'.54—dc20   92-1675

ISBN 0-393-03449-6

W. W. Norton & Company, Inc., 500 Fifth Avenue, New York, N.Y. 10110
W. W. Norton & Company Ltd., 10 Coptic Street, London WCIA 1PU

1 2 3 4 5 6 7 8 9 0

For Gail & Charoula

PART ONE

CHAPTER 1

IN 1970, ON the south side of Union, Ohio, Junior Johnson embalmed bodies, so he knew it was a lie about people being the same inside. In fact, everyone was different, even more different than you would think. Pretty women with unlined faces had brown clotted blood and mouths that fell open like doors when they died. Big men in plaid suits deflated like rag dolls when their spirits were gone—Junior had to stuff their small forms with rags; newspaper rustled too much. But it was the whites who were most frightening—across the board, whoever they were, they shrank up and took on the ice blue cast of ghosts when they passed on. Junior hated to see this, and usually didn't, since most whites took the trouble to drive thirty miles to the other funeral home on the outskirts of town. Unless there was a mistake and they didn't know that the sign saying JOHNSON AND JOHNSON meant Junior and his black father and two grandfathers before him. Unless they didn't know that he, Junior Johnson, standing at the door with his close-cropped pumpkin hair and burnished skin, was black all right and thought instead that he was Latin or Just Back from Florida, or didn't think at all, because who thought at times like that, with a body on your mind?

Junior took the whites, of course, he'd take anybody, and studying them had been a hobby since he was a child. To have one on ice, so to speak—to have a whole gray-faced family at his mercy, falling for the most blatant sales tactics ("Course, if you don't think your mother deserves the deluxe casket, you can always move to the next model down") gave him a thrill.

His own people rarely fell for such maneuvers and even more rarely had seven thousand squirreled away for a cherry casket that matched some wife's dining room set. No neighbor of his would agonize about having a favorite color for the lining or argue over the corpse's style of dress.

It took money, and money in your background, to have stupid concerns like that. And Junior had respect for the plain pine coffins, some thin as fruit crates, that he kept in a separate room in the back for his regular clientele—for the poor, the middle-poor, and the elderly. His neighborhood customers didn't even cry much in the cold showroom. Most of them knew their loved ones were tired; most of them knew one box was as good as the next. Junior had to keep his sales tricks in his pocket when his own people came around. He'd even talked down several of the exceptions—like the man down the street, wild with grief last month when a wife he'd neglected was hit and killed by a car.

"You haven't even paid off your Buick," Junior told

him. "What're you gonna look like spending five grand on a coffin?"

Junior could not keep himself from making these profit-ruining observations. People thanked him later, when they came out from under the miasma of grief, while he sometimes wanted to kick himself soundly in the butt. He got notes from folks as far away as Minneapolis, as long as a year after a death.

"You're a gentleman, Mr. Johnson," one woman wrote. "I'd be ruined if you hadn't talked me out of my foolishness."

"It's nice to know there are men who put honor before profit," someone's daughter from Washington, D.C. said.

Junior liked the word *honor* and kept that note in a bureau by his bed.

Junior had two assistants, Naomi and James, who had gone to mortuary school in Cleveland, but like Mr. Hyde, he liked to keep the occasional white until night, for himself. Then he could arrange lips and eyes, using pins and ghoulish plastic devices. Then he was in control of the countenance of people who wouldn't have given him the time of day during their lives. Even he, Junior B. Johnson the Fourth, with deeds in his lockbox and calves strong as rock, would have received only the slightest of glances from this Mrs. James Holmes, for example, with her liver lips and wattled neck, who had just arrived after suffering a coronary while attending a local Bible conference with her niece.

Junior didn't need to experience the life force in this

woman to feel that he knew who she was. She'd pulled a face of distaste long enough that it was etched at her mouth, along with a long wincing line down her brow. Her hands were curled shut as if she were trying to protect some treasure, and when Junior pried them open, they released a foul and intimate scent. She was carefully deodorized under her hairless arms and heavily perfumed at the neck, but the rest of her smelled corrupted, untended.

Most nights, there were two or three bodies in various stages of afterlife in the house on 37 Park Street, and the more there were, the more Junior liked it. Most everyone he knew in the black community eventually ended up in these rooms, and he often thought this, especially when he saw fast young men who'd gotten big too quickly, from women or drugs.

"Be seeing you soon, little brother," Junior said to himself when he drove by one on the streets, and sure enough, there he'd be, not a year later, stiff as an oak plank, already done.

He felt different about the old people who counted on him. Years before their deaths, elderly women called to tell him exactly how long they wanted the casket lid to be open, or how they wanted a cross lying, just so, across their chests. Junior kept a book of these details, a green leather diary of last desires. These old people didn't have family, or didn't trust them when it came to final matters of style.

It was through this realm of death and the anticipation of it that Junior had learned everything he knew about people. It all came out when you died, or were about to die, or when you lost someone. He'd seen the meanest men weep like toddlers, slobbering drool, when their mothers were gone; he'd seen the most beautiful women shrivel up like boneless birds. Uncovering the bodies of women had been one of the revelations of Junior's life. Who would have known how much artifice was involved in what you saw? The binding undergarments that once removed gave way to the sway of unsuspected flesh; the wig that hid a balding skull. Who would have thought that you could wash off a woman's eyebrows, that you could smear away the shape of her mouth? Reducing a woman to her true dimensions was for Junior an always sobering experience, and he marveled at what all of them, young and old, expended on how they looked. Men usually looked like who they were—only their plaids and stripes disguised them. But even the oldest of women arrived on the day of death showing some effort at allurement, a swipe of lipstick before the ambulance came, a chip of pink varnish on the tips of gnarled toes. (In Mrs. Holmes's case, the oil of lilacs, surely an enticement to someone, seemed kneaded into her flesh.) The pity Junior felt each time upon observing this flooded his throat, for he also knew the other truth about women from being in business so long—that underneath the accessories and ornament, you usually hit rock.

He had known many a man who got drunk at the Hi Life on the day of a baby's funeral; who disappeared to Cleveland on unexplained business when a father finally died. But women, underneath their flowered hats, baked cakes and showed up.

His own mother had arranged her cremation the day before she died and now stood where she had requested—in the living room, once hers, now Junior's, in an orange vase, near a south window, in the sun.

"And don't ever look at me!" she told Junior, and of course because she'd warned him, he had. He'd only been twenty years old at the time and she had been right to warn him. What could you believe in after you'd seen a beloved mother reduced to a few cupfuls of shard and ash? Junior had never been able to discover the answer to that.

Growing up, whenever Junior studied anyone, he thought about how they'd look when they died—he imagined them immobilized in a casket, their jaws slack, their hands arranged on their chests.

One of his first memories was of the corpse of Mabel Jones, a local soprano, decked out in pink—pink shoes, pink gloves, even a pink pillbox hat that his father had stapled to her wig. Junior must have just learned to walk, because he remembered laboring his way up the aisle to see this woman, nestled black and pink in the scalloped frills, like a candy, stumbling in front of a heart-shaped wreath of mums that spelled out MOM.

He must have known how to talk as well—or perhaps he imagined saying to Mabel Jones, her face as big as the iron skillet on which his mother fried eggs, "C'mon. Wake up!"

14

He remembered his father laughing at his antics. He enjoyed people, even people in his family, making fools of themselves, but eventually Junior's mother rescued him from the front of the room, swept him up in her perfumed arms, covered with a cool and watery silk.

"She's sleeping for good, honey," she whispered into his mouth, filling him with the wind of her peppermint breath; she smelled like this, without the aid of gum or mints, as if she had some internal source of freshness, right up until her death.

Junior spent his childhood watching his father drain blood from veins in the neck. He grew up with flattened hands, vanished arms, heads mysteriously detached. He was amazed at how many people survived, given their thin skins and watery interiors. The body was a poor, cheap thing; even a plastic cup could outlast it. He couldn't believe how many people relaxed, sitting on stoops, smoking cigarettes in the sun. Didn't they know a bolt of lightning, a fallen wire, an aneurysm could appear and finish them, for good?

In such a precarious world, Junior never learned to relax. Given a stray moment, he added sums in his mind; he sang stanzas of songs or typed out words on his thigh—his mother had made him take typing when he was young, hoping he would break out of the family mold and become an accountant.

No such sensitivity had ever plagued Junior's father, who saw the funeral business—who saw life—as a great, grand scam. He raked in the money with gusto, telling Junior, "Whites have been doing this for years!" He laughed over corpses and relished working on someone he didn't like. "I knew I'd get you," he'd say to the body of some gambler who'd betrayed him, or a woman who'd done him wrong—he'd had mistresses of all shapes and hues, all his life. Junior only saw him grow solemn over dead babies or particularly young and winsome women, in the latter case because they had died before he'd had his chance.

Yet in spite of his melancholy nature, Junior managed to steer himself through most of the expected stations of life. He graduated high school and stood at the front of a Baptist church among lilies and was married like anyone else; he sang hymns on Sunday, as if he believed someone were appreciating them. He sired a daughter, made money and saved it, but at some point that he could not always remember he had disappointed himself.

By the time his father died and left him the business, Junior, at thirty, had tried the navy, the coast guard, the Ford plant; he was disillusioned enough to accept. Everyone said it would be such a shame if he didn't; no one wanted to see a new sign.

He began to stand out on the porch on summer evenings like his grandfathers before him, an ear cocked for ambulances, poised for people to die. He didn't have a long wait. Union was full of old folks who toppled over like elms. With Junior's era, however, guns and drugs entered town. There were great head and chest wounds, caused by bullets that exploded when they entered flesh. Junior was stumped and dismayed by these wounds, which he could neither alter nor disguise. And he decided not to disguise them—not to attend a seminar in Toledo that taught techniques for just this kind of problem. After years of watching his family disguise death, Junior rebeled, and caused an uproar when he first displayed a woman who had been shot without camouflaging her wounds. The woman's daughter fainted in front of the casket, and the husband, drunk and horrified, challenged Junior to a fight.

"Hey, I didn't shoot her!" Junior said when he walked out with the man to the street. He knew there would be no fight—grief took the fight right out of you; this man was as weak as a child. "You should have told me to close the box."

"Oh, man, did you see her?" the man cried, leaning against a telephone pole.

"I saw her, I saw her. I'm sorry," Junior said.

He had no son to prime for the business, and barely a daughter, but he was just as glad. He saw that his family had been involved in a disservice, not a service, all their lives, soothing people with pickled bodies arranged on sumptuous beds. They had been lying to customers, for profit, and whether they wanted to be lied to or not wasn't the point. Junior began to understand the exact form of the vague reason he hadn't wanted this profession, even as a boy. He had desired truth, and none of his patrons could stand it.

The evening of Mrs. Holmes's arrival, 37 Park Street held only two bodies, and one of them, Junior, couldn't settle down. He drank bourbon and water, he counted money, but none of these usual occupations helped. As if in a trance, he wandered to the bookshelf in his study and pulled out his yellowed high school yearbook, which fell open to the faculty section. Junior only turned one page, and there she was: Mrs. James Holmes, a hundred years younger and with a different name, Miss Edith Hutt, Miami University, Bachelor of Arts. The same livery lips and mottled neck, even then. Now that he saw her, he remembered everything about that year when she'd taught him English; 1939 fanned out with facts. He had been the only black in the class excepting so-called retarded twins, Terry and Jerry Roberts, who stayed on for years after Junior graduated and were finally relegated to a semi-permanent state called special education. Junior had been eighteen and literature had excited him that year for the first and last time. But Miss Edith had taken care of that; she'd nipped that in the bud. He remembered her static notes on his theme books that he had covered with black ink from a fountain pen of his father's: "Stick to the topic! Don't ramble. What is your point?" Whatever Junior had to say about Shakespeare, about Chaucer, about Melville, it wasn't clear, it wasn't so, and it was usually too much. His very words seemed to annoy Miss Edith. When he wrote Ph.D. on a questionnaire she sent around asking for vocational plans, she had approached him with a bemused curl on her horrid lips and asked, "Ph.D. in what?"

"English," Junior had answered flatly, not even sure what such a degree involved, but still at the end of a stage when he would state anything, hope anything, as long as it wasn't in the footsteps of his father.

"Junior requires more realistic goals," she wrote on his progress report that semester, a semester when she had veered off the track of literature entirely and given impassioned lectures—demented lectures, Junior thought—on global communism and the John Birch Society, and the roots and valor of the Ku Klux Klan.

Some poor man named Holmes must have eventually married her—Junior was amazed at how the most horrible people always found a mate—and Miss Edith eventually graced their town with her departure, but not before leaving on others, or at least on Junior, a deep, dark blot. He'd never read again like he had before she had scribbled across his thoughts. He had surely never written Ph.D. again, in his life. He could see that abbreviation now, written out of hope and ignorance, in 1939.

Miss Edith's entourage, a cluster of old women in ermine and button earrings, arrived later that evening to choose her coffin. Junior led them through the dimly lit rooms and watched them struggle with their consciences until they decided on what Junior thought was one of the uglier models—bright red satin, nestled in mahogany, six thousand and thirty-five dollars. All of these women, except for the niece, were fresh from Kokomo, Indiana, and had booked rooms at the Ramada Inn on the outskirts of town. At their request, Junior recommended a restaurant and saw in their faces as he

gave directions to plates of turkey and mealy potatoes
the growing realization that they were looking at someone black. He saw it in one woman particularly, who
wore white gloves and had a gnarled, nutlike head. Her
tiny eyes peered out at him, and he could see them
change, in the center, as he talked. After they left, he
watched them stand in a clot on his front porch as they
took in the neighborhood they were in for the first time;
he saw them look back up at the old sign, with the
flaked paint, with the second J, in the second JOHNSON,
gone. He saw them hold on to each other by their wings
as they moved down the iced front steps to their dark,
late model car. And perhaps—he could not be sure—
he saw them look up and see him, behind the lace curtains, watching.

He wanted to call out, "I knew your Miss Edith, I
knew her well." He wanted to find his old theme
papers—but, of course, he couldn't find them, he didn't
have them—and lay out on his dining room table the
pathetic old-fashionedness of his once-fervent words.
He wanted someone to see—and these white women in
particular—what he once had, and what had been lost.
But they would not have known what he was talking
about.

His wife, Helene, hadn't known either. For twenty
years, she had coaxed him out of the black moods that
gathered around him like a shawl—and then she had
gone. Junior had not believed that she would leave him;
it was a greater shock to him than if she'd simply lain
down and died. But Helene, who had wept the greater

bulk of her life away on him, who had lost weight, then gained it, then lost it again, all based on the state of his melancholy, had in the end displayed great strength in the legs and neck and spine. She had lifted herself out of the maroon velvet chair where she had sat most of their married life, and that frame of hers had held her up and moved her out.

What she had complained about over the years—his hermit life, his quietness, the stench of embalming fluids on the clothes he often didn't bother to change—grew worse after she was gone. Now there was no one to note them, no one except his brown dog, who loved him anyhow.

"Junior Johnson's gone strange"—he heard people saying this around town, because he still went out when he had to, for food, for bourbon, for cruises around the neighborhood. He noticed that some people seemed scared of him—he often drove the old hearse instead of his Buick—and they looked at him driving by as if he were death itself. Children ran down alleys—he had seen them do this!—when they saw him coming in his big black gas-guzzling car.

He often drove out to the Walnut Grove Cemetery on the outskirts of town and studied the great stone angels the rich had drilled with verse and the above-ground mausoleums that the even richer situated on rolling hills with a view. Just like in town, there was a black section, and Junior preferred sitting there, with the flat markers in gray stone, most of them fallen down. There were no urns with plastic mums here and fewer wreaths of dried flowers. But he preferred this plain display, as he preferred the cheap coffins. BELOVED MOTHER, these stones said simply; DEPARTED SISTER. They didn't bother with poetry; it cost too much.

When Helene had lived with him, she had kept the funeral business out of the house. She had made Junior take his mortuary magazines out of the living room; she had first hung a curtain, then commissioned a door between the front rooms and the back, where the bodies were kept. She said she couldn't stand the smell of death that permeated the house, and she sprayed a floral air freshener every evening through all the rooms. She couldn't stand the silence and kept on the radio all the time, a low, constant murmuring of weather reports and hog prices, a man's voice that never stopped.

But Helene wasn't here now—Junior wasn't even sure where she was—and the door remained open, the rooms silent, the smell of the air sweet and odd. Every once in a while Junior's brown dog scratched its fleas and there was the metallic sound of rattling chain. Occasionally a car swished by on the wet street, or the refrigerator—mostly empty now except for cold cuts—moaned, as if bereft.

The only music Junior ever listened to came from a black radio station out of Nashville that switched on blazingly at 9:00 P.M., cutting off in midverse a local Baptist station with limited funds. This rocking, honky-tonk music reminded him of a time before he'd been a husband or a mortician or anything for that matter, just a light-skinned black man with a fine head and a long, loose-limbed body. He'd gone to dance clubs during this period, the year after high school graduation, the year after Mrs. Holmes, when he had thought—to hell with it then, to hell with it all. He had gone to the back rooms of barbeque restaurants, and girls in pastel dresses had swarmed around him like mosquitoes and lit on his arm. He steered them around the floor with the lightest of pressure, and they moved their hips and looked up into his face and he felt charmed.

He had entertained the illusion that this might be his life—a princely, decadent existence, where he slept till noon and his mother folded his underwear, and pork chops materialized on the dinner table each evening, peppery and fried. But then his father appeared in his doorway one evening when Junior was dressing in a blue pastel suit with black piping around the collar and said, "I want to see a paycheck. In a week," and backed out again.

It was all right, Junior decided; he'd only been masquerading anyhow; he never had the stomach to actually seduce one of the girls at the dance club, for example. He had been cursed with an awareness of anatomy—he would fixate on a girl's clavicle or the long bones in her arms. It was not a successful fixation, romancewise, and he was already gathering a reputation for being odd when Helene came along. The only reason he had gone so far with her was that she wore sleek, long-sleeved dresses and insisted on discourse instead of love.

Still, now that she'd left him, Junior sometimes

moved to this music in front of the mirror in the hall. He could still do certain steps, as outdated as they might be now. He had only stopped doing this lately, after Naomi had walked in on him one day when he was doing a shambling two-step to a gospel song.

"Mr. Johnson!" she said, and he stopped in his tracks, aware that he couldn't pretend this scene was other than it was: he was a grown man in a bathrobe being serenaded by the Five Blind Boys of Alabama and shaking his hips in a fashion that was at least twenty years old.

Night had fallen after Mrs. Holmes's friends departed, as if they had left it to him as a gift—or a curse. Junior usually welcomed the night—he felt guilty during the day that he wasn't out more in the world. Night was when he went into his backrooms and worked.

Miss Edith was still lying there, of course. He didn't know what he'd hoped. She was still there, covered with a sheet, on the stainless steel table, a tag around her foot. Seventy-nine years old, white female, myocardial infarction, December 10th showing, the tag said, in Junior's hand. He had written it only this afternoon, years ago, when he hadn't known who she was.

Junior drew back the sheet and looked at her again. Somewhere in the coil of her brain was embedded the old boy he once was—in a white shirt and tweed jacket, with leather patches at the elbows. Miss Edith had been the last one to see him like this, since, in effect, she had killed him. She'd been the last to note that particular, and limited, gold ardor in his eyes. Something in this brain, under this face that he studied now, had been triggered by some element in him and had wanted to squash it.

Looking at the purpling body of Miss Edith in the dusty house on Park Street, Junior desired more than he had ever desired anything to have back his young self.

Miss Edith's showing was late; her group had arrived early, after a country breakfast at the Ramada that had left their stomachs queasy—they agreed in the car on the way over that pancakes first thing were just too much—and they had each filed into Junior's tiny public bathroom and spent a prolonged time flushing the toilet, until they all gathered again, faces even whiter than usual, in their pastel gloves and hats. Although Junior had let them in, he had disappeared entirely after that. They looked at their little watches, gold and silver Timexes that ticked off the exact same time. They had adjusted them on the trip from Indiana, along with rearranging their purses and billfolds; now they didn't know what to do with themselves.

In the Sunday morning daylight, Junior's establishment revealed itself in all its shabbiness—their women's eyes were pulled to the corners, where spiderwebs not only hung, but had actual spiders on them.

"He must be a widower," the niece whispered to the others as they adjusted waistbands and belts—the pancakes seemed to be expanding in them. Finally, when

25

Junior still didn't appear, they sat with soft sighs on the upholstered chairs in the lobby, dusty, floral chairs that could have used a good scrubbing. They crossed and recrossed their tight legs, encased in stockings. They slipped off the patent leather pumps, decorated girlishly with bows and contrasting stripes and, in the case of the niece, large mock rhinestones. They sat, patient and impatient at the same time—each had waited unhappily through long periods of her life—and eventually dipped down into the reservoir of their own private thoughts. A few thought of their own deaths, hoping they would not end up in such a godforsaken place. Another worried over a husband back home, elderly and childlike, blundering through his meals alone. No one thought of Miss Edith—Mrs. Holmes to them—except in annoyance. It was just like her to die so inconveniently, in her old hometown so many miles away, and then to have done so near such a bad neighborhood. They had already discussed how Miss Edith, a famous bigot, would turn over in her grave if she knew where she'd ended up— in this black man's ramshackle funeral home. But of course she wasn't in the grave yet, and as far as they could tell she might know all about it, given what was being written in magazines nowadays about after-death awareness. She was a know-it-all, Miss Edith, and it would be just like her to be sniffing around disapprovingly even now.

None of the women, except for the niece, was sure how she'd been roped into serving in this capacity for Miss Edith, who had complained and badgered and ma-

ligned her way through life. But there had been connections, and they had to be honored. One woman was
her neighbor; the other a sister of her poor, embattled,
now dead husband, James; the other was a member of
her church who used to pick her up on Sundays.

The niece thought privately that it was lucky Edith
had died with her in Union, where a branch of the old
Hutt family, all dead now, had a family plot. It was a
good excuse for not shipping back the body, a costly,
complex operation; it was an even better excuse for the
small turnout. Few people would have come to see
Edith, even back in Indiana, just a few strays like these,
aimless on a Sunday after church, who would have
headed to the funeral parlor simply to see who was
showing.

Junior washed, then rewashed his silver instruments,
his hands, the counter, dawdling, dawdling. He could
not bear the thought of those white pearl heads out in
his parlor—they reminded him of onions. He couldn't
actually believe what he had done. He felt the way a
murderer must feel, but of course there had been no life
in these backrooms for ages, except for his own. When
Naomi had shown up an hour ago, he had turned her
away at the front door, but not before noting her long,
lowering look at his white shirt, stained by a stripe of
blood.

"Are you all right, Mr. Johnson?" she asked him,
because he often didn't seem all right now.

"Sure, I'm all right," Junior said unconvincingly.

"I've paid you, haven't I? Did I give you your check?"

"I'm paid up," Naomi said, backing up. "I didn't even work last week, remember?"

"Oh, right. Well, never mind. It's been pretty slow." Junior followed her gaze to his chest and swiped at the blood, which smeared and looked even more hideous. *Hideous*—that was the word for the day, Junior thought. Naomi turned around, shaking her head, and walked to her brand-new red car, and Junior was dazed enough to find himself wondering how she could afford it—he certainly didn't pay her enough. She backed out quickly, almost hitting a cottonwood on the corner of his lot. He stood there far too long, till the carload of Miss Edith's comrades pulled up. Then he'd had to run into the back room and change his shirt and wash himself and return with his false smile to let them in to smell up his bathroom—their scent, of elimination and eau de cologne, seeped all the way into the back.

He couldn't wait much longer; he'd have to go out and face them, face the music—that was a saying his mother had used before she died. He combed his hair and noted his trembling hands, which he would have to keep in his pockets. He sniffed at his armpits, from which sweat had been pouring out all morning, but he smelled of the freshness of his clean shirt, steamed at the laundry down the street—he was surrounded in its crisp aromatic scent. On the way to the door, he stopped at his bookshelf and took out a well-thumbed book by Norman Vincent Peale, *The Power of Positive Thinking*. He had been contemptuous of this book when he was a boy—it had been a favorite of his father's—and he remembered scanning it back when he was lost in *Beowulf* and *Hamlet*, scornful of its thin advice. But now he ruffled the pages frantically, hoping for something he could use right now. But the words swam in front of him, a gray lake, and all he could think of was that he'd heard somewhere that it did you good to smile, that the actual act of smiling involved muscles that thereby triggered some positive mechanism—where? In the brain, Junior supposed, but he didn't want to think about that now. He worked his mouth up—it was as painful as doing a chin-up—and opened the door.

"We thought you'd forgotten us." The niece spoke up when she saw him, with her own bogus smile. She was the boldest—the youngest, too—and the other women were glad of her nerve.

"I'm sorry," Junior said. "I'm a little behind. If you would follow me, please."

He did not wait for the older women to get their balance after sitting so long; he was in the parlor before them and quickly lit a candelabra in front of Miss Edith's coffin. He stood reverentially there in front of it and felt the force of the group of white women as they gathered behind him, tearless and quiet, breathing through their mouths. Junior stood for what seemed an eternity, lost in the gleam of mahogany, the play of light on the dark box. Finally he turned back around—that wan smile again—and tried to retreat with a courtly little bow.

"Why isn't the casket open?" The bold one, the niece, snagged him as he passed.

29

"There were no provisions for that in my instructions," Junior managed, his hands deep in his pockets, which were filled with lint and dead matches.

"Provisions?" the sister-in-law repeated, as if the word itself were an outrage.

"I mean that it's not customary to have an open casket ceremony unless arrangements are made beforehand," Junior said.

"What arrangements are needed?" the niece asked. "Just open it. We want to see my aunt."

Junior smiled again, and it was altogether the most painful act of his life. He had handsome teeth—his best asset, as far as looks went—but they felt as if they were on fire.

"I'm afraid that's impossible."

The neighbor of Mrs. Holmes stepped forward in her peach acetate skirt and blouse—stepped forward for one of the first times in her life. "Impossible? What do you mean impossible? In Indiana we're not put through such rigamarole." Her face matched her skirt, matched her iced hair, an unnatural color that Junior knew no human woman, white or not, could actually own.

"There was actually some difficulty in the embalming process. This sometimes happens. I'm afraid your Mrs. Holmes is not presentable. Please take my word for this, ladies. I wouldn't want you to be subjected."

The women gasped, in unison, and between them managed more feeling for Miss Edith in that instant, in imagining her mutilation, than they had worked up for her during her long years of life. After the gasps there

30

were tears, and Junior escaped while they were fumbling around in their purses for hankies.

He returned to the backroom covered in a sheen of sweat and closed the door with a satisfying click. What could they do to him, what could they ever do to him, now that he was himself again? He relaxed his smile and opened a window near the gray mass floating in a beaker of formaldehyde on his shelf, but even with a breeze there was still everywhere the scent of lilacs.

CHAPTER 2

DRIPPING WET ON the west side of Union, Louis Dardio weighed in at eighty-eight and one-half pounds. He knew this because he soaked himself down in the shower every morning to check, hoping that the accumulation of Zero bars and Almond Mounds and Hersheys with Almonds he consumed would push him over the hundred mark. He thought one hundred was a good weight to be, that it was the minimum before you could stop being a boy. And he was ready to stop being one any time now. He had high hopes that the next, heavier stage of himself would be better.

This was not a hope fostered by his older sister, Loretta, however. She had moaned loudly when she hit that mark on the scales and made him promise not to tell anyone, thereby giving him the idea to do just that to Darrell Lutes, one of the lanky boys who had begun idling by their cement stoop ever since Loretta had hit puberty with a bang. No one had ever hung out on the stoop for Louis; he had to find his own friends. And

33

next to other boys his age, with their badger faces and roped arms, he felt thin, short, clumsier than ever—and most of all light. Whenever he tried to do all the things he was supposed to do in conjunction with them—to compete, for example—he hurt himself.

"Why's everything so hard for you two?" his mother protested when Louis returned home with some injury from his ineptness. They were odd injuries to top it off; once a basketball hoop had fallen off a neighbor's garage and hit him in the eye.

His mother said these things when Loretta was simultaneously suffering in one of the many mirrors that someone in his family had foolishly installed throughout their house. You couldn't go anywhere without encountering your physical self, an awful prospect for Louis, who thus could not even be in his own home without perpetually encountering inferiorities that seemed locked in the bone. What were the chances that his head would ever grow, for example, or that his spindly knees would ever flesh out?

The great abundance of reflective surfaces was even worse on his sister; ever since her thirteenth birthday, she had mooned over one or another version of herself, all dire. Louis had developed a listing gait, an averted eye as he moved through their rooms, but Loretta looked straight at herself, endlessly, and every week something was wrong.

"I can't do anything with my hair!"

"My skin's a mess!"

"How'd I get to be so fat!"

Although she had vowed never to speak to Louis after his treachery with Darrell Lutes, she still said these things to him whenever he was unfortunate enough to be passing by.

"You look fine," he usually muttered, because the one time he had actually told her the truth—that she did look chubby in the dirndl skirt she had on—she hadn't left him alone. "Really chubby—or just a little chubby? Would you have noticed if I hadn't brought it up?"

Louis had finally gone to their mother for assistance—his sister seemed nearly mad to him at that moment—but all she had said was, "Can't either of you be normal?" His mother was no help, he saw. In fact, it must have been something his family had or had not taught him and his sister that made them the way they were.

Louis often wished for an older brother to lead him sagely around. Sisters were useless, especially one at another stage than you. He and Loretta had only been close back in a time he could barely remember now, when they didn't even know what they looked like, when their mother dressed them like objects and pushed them about and sat them up, like salt and pepper shakers, in the backseat of the family car. Since then Loretta had shot ahead of him; she was three years older, and now always vacating whatever stage he was coming upon.

But lately word of her reputation in high school had begun trickling down. "You're *Loretta's* brother?" boys asked when he said his last name, and their eyes filled with some brown, awful knowledge at his nod.

At first, Louis thought it must be sex, that Loretta did it, whatever it was, and he had his ideas. It had to do with the bulky boxes in the linen closet that said SANITARY on the lid; it had to do with what was under her padded bra, which collapsed gently if you brushed into her by mistake, with what she planned to elicit with the cloying Yardley perfume she sprayed on her hair and neck. This scent wafted down from her bedroom, turning left through the living room, then right again into the kitchen, where it sometimes assailed him as he sat at the table working on his plate of bland macaroni and cheese (their mother used Velveeta and margarine, no salt). His sister's scent took his appetite away, but he ate; otherwise, he would be grounded.

Grounding was his mother's last ammunition against Loretta, and lately she had extended the threat to him. Louis thought it sounded like an electrical term, something to do with shortages. Their grandfather was an electrician, and Louis had often stood listlessly with him in his basement, hoping to be inspired by the manly— and dirty—surroundings: the dead radios and coils of wire and dastardly looking tools. But their mother's particular kind of grounding punished only them. To have Loretta trapped in their small rooms when she didn't want to be there, her swollen perfumed presence clanking about, made their house seem volatile, unbearable, as if the roof might explode off them all.

"What else can I do?" he heard their mother say on the phone to someone, possibly another mother on their block. She had grown up in Gilbert, a town even smaller than this one, and had married their father in what seemed an inevitable stage of her development, as if marriage were the next component after growing wisdom teeth and graduating high school. Louis assumed —he hoped—that she had been untouched by anyone else.

It was easier for them to release his sister, to open the screen door and let her out like a moth on those nights when she stormed and swore. The calm after her exit felt cool on the back of Louis's neck as he sat with the remains of his family in front of the wavering TV. His teeth ached when she was there, and his palate was dry at her departure. There was more to this than sex, he was afraid.

> *Don't send me no doctor,*
> *To fill me up with all those pills*
> *Got me a man named Doctor Feel Good*
> *And Oh! That man takes care of all my pains*
>   *and all my ills.*

This is what Loretta listened to on the tiny record player that, if Louis remembered correctly, had been given to them both. Music had never been a component of their family life, although they had all been briefly excited when their father had brought home a cherry hi-fi set and placed it in the center of their living room. This was one of their father's roles, it seemed, to purchase large items that could not be easily handled and to place them at their feet.

And although their mother played the record that accompanied the hi-fi ("Johnny Mercer's All Time Favorites"), after a few weeks it sat stolid and silent, almost a reproach.

But at night when Louis didn't know what to do with himself, when he had gone through his piles of comics and their suggestive party tricks in the back (these seemed antiquated to Louis, who had never been to a party in his life. But perhaps in New York City, where these items were manufactured, raucous groups of people met together and used whoopee cushions and X-ray glasses and black gum to enliven their time), he sat in front of the hi-fi and turned the glowing knob. Despite its bulk, the radio didn't pick up much more than his little Japanese transistor—an electrical gift from his grandfather. The farthest you could reach was Detroit to the north, with its double weather forecasts of Ontario, and to the south WLAC, a black Nashville station that featured Randy's Record Mart and groups like Little Jimmy and the Soul Stirrers.

Loretta also liked the Nashville station, which transmitted only late when tamer channels had been put to bed. One night on her way out, she stopped and listened with Louis to advertisements for Silky Straight Hair Relaxer and Red Rose Skin Bleaching Creme. "Lighten and Brighten," the last jingle went.

"Imagine, wanting to change your color," she said in a wondering voice, not necessarily to him, he felt. Louis rarely saw her like this anymore, without her mask of ornamental seductiveness. But noting her at all ruined his furtive pleasure, and he raised his hand to the knob.

"Leave it a minute," she said and stood beside him, her high-heeled shoes an inch from his head, as they listened to a man named Johnny Taylor sing "Who's Making Love to Your Old Lady While You're Out Making Love?"

Louis's ears burned, either from the lyrics or from the thought "She could kick me," which rose, unbidden, in his mind. She didn't, of course. She was his sister, after all.

Louis's family moaned whenever opera singers appeared between ventriloquists and comedians on the "Ed Sullivan Show"; they moaned but did not rise to turn them off. Louis smirked along with the rest of them, but in truth the music shook him, especially the foreign cries of the short dark tenors—he would look like this someday, he thought.

Louis wanted music, but there seemed to be no place for it in his family. And it certainly couldn't be found where you'd expect it—in the junior high school orchestra, for example, where he'd somehow found himself playing a horn. He thought it was sheer lack of talent that had made his mother link him with a trumpet; anyone with lips could technically blow one. She insisted both he and Loretta learn something musical, not so much for the sounds they made, but as a discipline that would translate itself later into other realms—such as getting up at dawn and going off to a job you didn't like.

He practiced fitfully in the basement on a slightly corroded model his father had commandeered from somewhere, trying for a time when no one was home, or his mother was at least in the rec room, lost in the intrigues of her soap opera. When Loretta was there, he remained poised for her inevitable complaint. "Headache," she called down the basement stairs at his screeching. "You're causing a major headache up here."

She had long ago given up playing the oboe, for which she had shown a surprising talent. Their mother was annoyed about the discarded instrument, now dismembered in its vinylette case in the coat closet next to the laundry chute, where they shoved down their soiled garments, as if to some fairy laundress—but Loretta did not care. This was her favorite phrase, with variations: "I don't care"; "Who cares?"; "I could care less," which Louis knew didn't make sense. It should have been "I *couldn't* care." But his sister was not interested in grammatical correction, nor in "Red River Valley" or "Edelweiss," the kind of tunes favored by the Union High School Band. Surely there was no oboe part in existence for the James Brown forty-five she was playing on this white day in November 1969—a grinding, tribal, exhilarating song. "I break out . . . in a cold sweat," the voice called down the carpeted stairs of her room, and Louis, passing by, was so obedient that he did so, at the mere suggestion.

One of the tales in his family was how Loretta would have been named Karl had she been a boy. Why Louis hadn't subsequently been called this was never made clear. Had there been something about his newborn visage that had suggested his own antique name? Surely a name shackled you to certain possibilities as much as DNA. His sister's name, for example, suggested languorousness, and separation by syllables. "Lucious Loretta" he'd heard a boy call her once, but his sister did not seem to aim for anything as sheer as that.

Earlier that afternoon when he'd picked up the kitchen extension, not to call anyone but to see who was on the party line, he had heard a man saying her name, among much else. Something indefinable in this man's voice suggested a neighborhood, a heritage, other than their own.

"I been waiting for you, Loretta. What are you gonna do for me when you come?"

Loretta had seemed unable to say, or Louis hadn't been able to bear to hear it; before there was more, he'd hung up in the delicate way he had perfected for party line eavesdropping.

The calls he listened in to were much less scintillating and were punctuated by long female silences.

"What're you doing?"

"Nothing."

"When's he coming?"

"Later."

"How're you feeling?"

"All right."

No one said, "I'm getting into my car and driving to Canada," although it was right there, waiting to be driven to. No one said, "I'm stabbing my husband," or "I'm shaving off every hair on my head."

These conversations were so bland and predictable that Louis sometimes snorted into the receiver. So many *somedays* and *suppose sos*. He could sympathize with at least this about his sister—when she stomped in her high heels on the kitchen linoleum and shouted out "Now!"—she had *nows* in her at least; it made him hopeful that there was some spark in their lineage that he could bank on.

"What're you looking at?" Loretta asked him after dinner; she was standing in front of the hall mirror, back-combing the top of her hair. She had long wavy hair that she had decided in her perverse way was ugly. She had a talent for this, for taking everything she had—her large eyes, her wide hips, her swollen mouth—and ridiculing them until their beauty disappeared, even to you.

"Nothing," Louis said, averting his gaze.

He was sitting by the hi-fi, which he could only enjoy in her absence. She tossed her hair, then turned to look at her left flank, as if she thought it might soon be judged.

Their mother wandered into the living room.

"Where do you think you're going?" she asked Loretta.

"Out with Heather."

These were the words she said, but Louis heard "to meet a black man," as clear as a bell. His mother heard something too, Louis was sure of it. He felt he shouldn't witness this exchange, but what should he be doing exactly? Wasn't this his family's hi-fi, in his family's living room? Wasn't this his family, after all?

"You're not going anywhere," their mother said, but without much punch.

Loretta turned on her then—she looked a million feet taller in her high heels and bigger all over, because of her hair—and delivered one of the monologues common to this particular corridor of their house, the hallway leading from the mirror to the door. Louis noted the typical phrases without hearing their substance.

But it was their mother who surprised him; she must have talked to someone more potent than the housewives on their street for advice. When Loretta reached for her little purse (Louis was dying to see what was in it besides her lipstick, surely cigarettes and odious birth control devices), their mother spoke up. "You're grounded all month. If you go out tonight, I'm calling the police. There's a word for kids like you— *incorrigible*."

Loretta looked at Louis at the formal word, the way she had once looked at him when they were little and their parents had been especially foolish, when their father locked his car keys in their Buick or their mother toddled out of their cabin at the lake in her stiff floral bathing suit with a wide frilled skirt.

"Incorrigible? That's good. I haven't been called that one yet."

She moved past them both to the front door. "If you'd stoop to putting your own daughter in jail, go right ahead."

"You know all about stooping, don't you?" their mother muttered, and Loretta turned back and cried, "Racist!" as she slammed the door.

Such an ugly word, as bad as *rancid*; it hung in the room after she was gone. Louis lifted a trembling hand and turned on the hi-fi. Nashville was coming in strong tonight and was featuring the Dixie Hummingbirds, who sounded far off in some irretrievable past. He turned up the rocking music as his mother moved into the kitchen and picked up the phone.

Louis didn't know how he'd ever become so obedient, but it seemed easier than the opposite, the way Loretta was, for example. It wasn't that he didn't plan to rebel—he just didn't know against what yet. The stage he was at now, newly aware of his body, particularly the region below his neck, when his voice cracked and failed him and he woke in the middle of the night with a doomed feeling of expectation—surely this would soon pass.

"You'll get over it" was a favorite refrain of his parents, but what were you supposed to do with it while it was there?

So he *existed*; that seemed the right word for his low-level activity, when he felt on some provisional voltage not quite his own. He existed and he watched and listened, clearly more than anyone thought.

"What about Louis?" he heard one or another of his family ask, who knew in what context? And there would be no verbal answer, just the physical one he didn't see, but could feel, rooms away: a wave of the hand, a shrug. He didn't weigh enough yet to count.

Loretta, on the other hand, weighed too much. Her presence filled the house. If you flung a window open, something of her, her voice, her smell, her mammoth dissatisfaction, was sure to swell out. A separate wing could not have contained her. Why couldn't his parents see this? "Let her go!" he wanted to tell them, just as he had one of the boys on his block after he'd shown him a rabbit in a leghold trap. Louis had managed to help that creature escape at least, although its leg had been such a bloodied mangle that Loretta said it was sure to be killed by a predator.

"What's a predator of rabbits?" he had asked meanly, certain she wouldn't know. She hadn't—his family seemed void of facts, besides being musicless. He didn't know how any of them had made it this long.

And he had set other things free, whenever he had the chance. He was the one who secretly opened jam jars where neighborhood boys trapped lightning bugs and praying mantises, mollifying them with a few scraps of grass. And he had let butterflies go in biology once after everyone went to recess. They fluttered dumbly out the window, unaware that straight pins were planned for their tender flanks. Although his teacher had assured him that these creatures only lived a few days, Louis didn't care. He knew the answer his sister pretended not to—that human boys were the predators of everything, after all.

———

Loretta vowed to speak to no one in the family after her night in the county jail, but this was hard for her to manage. She was still a dependent, no more or less in the eyes of the law than Louis, who had suddenly taken such points of view into account. She had to ask for lunch money and panty hose money and makeup money (something about her always needed augmentation or camouflage), and surely asking was speaking, no matter how you looked at it.

This disappointed Louis; a true rebel wouldn't expect her parents to foot the bill for her mascara; a real revolutionary spirit (was this, he hoped, what his sister was?) would not appropriate outfits fashioned on their mother's rattling Singer for her own seditious purposes.

But this is what Loretta did—what she continued to do—even after her night in jail, an act that had obviously marked her, though not in the intended ways. (She'd only been detained for two and a half hours in the booking room, but not to hear her tell it. Louis heard her railing on her blue princess extension, "I was imprisoned by my own family!")

Once on her body, mild outfits that looked perfectly bland on the hanger were transformed into uniforms of seduction. He saw how she did some of this, how she rolled up skirts at the waistband and tucked in sweaters so they molded her curves. But it was simply her—her body—a way she had gathered around herself until it had become her identity.

The next week Louis had the misfortune of trailing a block behind his sister to school. He usually left much earlier, but he'd overslept because of a complicated dream in which he'd been saving a young woman from a house fire. Loretta usually got picked up anyway, if not at home, then at various strategic points along the way. She had luck—he had to give that to her—and many mornings Louis tromped through snow, burdened with every book he owned (he couldn't help himself, he studied), while his sister in her light attire and single spiral-bound notebook was swept off her high-heeled feet into some Buick or Dodge.

It was a red Mustang that stopped for her that day, a clear but cold one with wind that tore in silver sheets at Louis's face, and he had to contain the impulse to call out and chase after her, to get in himself. He'd had a sense that this particular car was going to pick her up as soon as it passed his line of sight. The driver was a man, there was no doubt of this—even when the car passed him at thirty miles an hour, Louis could tell. And it was a black man to top it off, of a certain category in Louis's mind. He leaned toward the center of his car as if reaching under the seat for something illicit, as if already murmuring to someone. This car was newish, at least, Louis thought, as he watched his sister climb into the passenger side, releasing into the cold wind of South Street a trail of cigarette smoke that hit him a moment later. She had been eyed by men in a variety of old and rusted autos that he would have hated to see her enter.

He was relieved that Loretta was oblivious to his presence, that she hadn't known he had been trailing her sturdy calves for several blocks as they passed the Wheel

Inn Restaurant and the back of the concrete real estate
office where their father sat with his monogrammed
handkerchiefs. The pickup—and his urge to follow
her—occurred squarely in front of Kugler's bakery, his
favorite spot along the way. He thought this location
was part of the reason for his urge to chase her, to claim
her, to scrunch up beside her familiar flesh in the black
man's car: all of South Street at this particular spot was
suffused with the tender aroma of rising bread.

Christmas arrived in the middle of this time, inap-
propriately, for no one in Louis's family felt like cele-
bration. November, then December, had been cold and
dark and dank, as if a tarnished bowl had been inverted
over their town.

Their mother's mimeographed holiday letter left out
everything important that year. The weather, then
Louis, were moved to the forefront for obvious reasons,
and he winced at her inflations:

> Louis now plays first horn in the or-
> chestra and has high hopes for getting on the
> basketball team this year. You wouldn't
> know him: five feet already and still grow-
> ing, if you use my clothes budget as a guide.

Louis imagined the real letter, the one he would
write, his voice spilling from his mother's hand:

Louis remains short; he will always be short; there seems little doubt of that now. He has no friends and no prospects for making any, and a girl has yet to notice him in his life. He gets As and Bs in school, seemingly without trying, but who cares about that?

Loretta has entered another realm; we're not sure what it is, but black people seem to be in it, and the most haunting, tribal music. She's picked up an accent from wherever she goes, and carries a smell underneath her perfume, like a layer of someone else's sweat. Whenever she's home, she sits in the sun in her wool coat, as if to bake something out of herself. She looks dreamy, stunned, goofy; also, sometimes, sad. If she is interested in anything other than her own reflection, we have no indication of it here.

Despite threats and vows and counterthreats, Loretta was almost never home now. She left in the morning with a totebag of beauty paraphernalia and returned late at night when everyone had flopped in exhaustion from wondering where she was. Whenever she opened her mouth, a lie, like a wafer, fell out.

"How was the dance?" their mother asked on one of the rare occasions when they were all up when she returned.

"The what?"

"The Y dance. Isn't that where you said you were going?"

"Oh, yeah. It was great. Real good," Loretta said, climbing her stairs. They all knew she was lying. She didn't even care what they thought.

They had eight more months of her before she went off to college, if, as their mother said, she made it that long. She made it sound as if Loretta might expire before that or disappear in some other way straight off the face of the earth. Louis tried to imagine a life, a house, without his sister in it, but he found it too hard. What would they contemplate without her?

In spite of his mother's upbeat version, Louis hadn't made the basketball team and didn't have a chance in hell of making it any year. Christmas passed dully, and the sun remained hidden, as if nothing in their region deserved illumination. Without light, in such a body, Louis felt as if he existed only to himself.

So he was surprised when a black man called out to him from an idling car the night after New Year's when he was returning home from delivering newspapers. (It was the *Herald News*, a useless rag of birth notices and local court news; throwing it on a stoop was more bother than it was worth, but his parents had insisted he do so, for reasons having to do with fortitude.)

"Say, do you happen to know Loretta Dardio?" the man called out.

Louis stopped, then backed up slowly, as if a mechanism in him had been thrown into reverse. Even talking to this man was a violation of a dozen creeds hammered into him, hammered into Loretta too, now that he thought of it, for all the good it had done. He backed up until he reached the window; it was the same red car that he had seen Loretta get into on South Street.

"Why?" he asked.

"Well, do you or don't you? I need to talk to her about something. She said her house number was eighty-six or eighty-seven, but I can't make out anything in the dark."

Louis saw that this wasn't entirely true—that this man also meant he couldn't very well stop in the middle of this very white neighborhood and go door to door, asking for Loretta—especially dressed as he was, all in red. He even had on a red hat—a rakish red hat, Louis thought, who often spent whole nights in the *Webster's* dictionary, pondering new words. No one black had ever even hesitated on his street, as far as Louis could remember, unless he was on the back of a garbage truck.

Louis wondered what would happen if he took this man home now, easy as you please, if he threw open the door and called out, "Loretta, there's a visitor for you."

Maybe his parents wouldn't even dislodge themselves from their nest of *TV Guides* and afghans. The man could go right on up to Loretta's room and do whatever he wanted. But Loretta wasn't home, of course. That she might have multiple contacts in this foreign world she mixed in set off a hum in Louis's head.

"She's not home," he managed at last, and the man smiled. He was a young man, Louis saw from his teeth. He'd never realized before how much you could tell from them. They were so white in the gray night that it looked as if a light had been switched on in his mouth.

"So you're her brother," the young man said, almost tenderly, Louis thought. "You kinda look like her, in the eyes."

Louis nodded; he had to keep himself from leaning into the car. This was the closest encounter of its kind he'd ever had, and he saw now why his sister was so fascinated. A low trickle of music spilled out of the car's rich interior, which looked upholstered in something beyond velvet, something sumptuous as fur. Louis couldn't make out the source of the music, which must have involved intricate speakers and wires. The word *wires* reminded him of his grandfather, white and oblivious, in another town, which in turn brought him back to his family.

"What do you want with her?" he asked.

The man was busy with something on the seat beside him—a gun, a knife? Louis wondered wildly. But it was only a Kleenex, a frail white flower of a Kleenex, like his grandmother tucked in her bodice. The young man blew his nose delicately—he had a cold, Louis saw.

"What do I want with her?" the young man asked after he wiped his nose. He had a friendly, casual tone. "Well, let's just say your sister and I are friends and that I wanted to talk to her about the kind of things friends talk about."

"Oh." Louis had to pee by now, and worse. Excitement did this to him. "Why don't you just call her?"

"I've tried that, but her mother"—the young man paused a second and smiled ruefully—"*your* mother, always seems to pick up the phone now and there's something about the way I sound."

Louis thought of the conversation he had overheard—*What're you gonna do for me when you come?*—and saw that it was possible his sister had been speaking to someone else. He had to keep himself from blurting this out, from telling how the princess extension in Loretta's room had been provisionally yanked out by their mother in a fit of rage, and then later more professionally disconnected by North Ohio Telephone.

He couldn't believe all the impulses he had to resist in this conversation—his mouth felt visibly swollen by all the things he couldn't—shouldn't—tell.

"I'd better go," he forced from his throat. He looked down at his paper bag, where two *Herald News* were nestled in the bottom. "You want a paper?"

The man took off his hat and leaned out the window, thus displaying himself for an instant, his tight cap of kinked hair, a stretch of walnut neck, eyelashes curled like Loretta's were after she trapped them for some moments in a silver device.

"Thanks, little brother, don't mind if I do."

Louis reached down and gave both of them to him, impetuously.

The young man held on to his end a moment until Louis looked up.

"Tell your sister Luther was looking for her, will you?"

Louis nodded numbly and backed off. Luther! It was as bad as his name; he couldn't believe how exhilarated he felt. He walked around the block in a daze, worried the young man would trail him home. He cut through backyards and parking lots until he was nearly lost himself.

Louis sneaked up to Loretta's room when she returned home at midnight, unable to keep the news to himself. Lying in bed, his body had beat with it; he felt as if he were solid heart.

"He what? Oh God! Tell me exactly what he said."

"That's all. 'Tell Loretta I was looking for her,' " Louis repeated for the third time. He was pleased to be the holder of so much information and to watch his sister work to extract it.

"Start from the beginning again. You were walking home . . ."

Louis talked, leaving out all the important things: the man's teeth, his mention of their mother, that moment when both of their hands were on the *Herald News*; he saw it was preferable to store up some things for yourself.

Loretta finally stopped pacing and sat down on the bed; without her makeup, she looked like her old sluggish self. "But was he actually going to come here?"

"He said you told him the house number."

"I did not! Oh, maybe I did. I was supposed to

meet him out south, but I was late because Sandy's car wouldn't start—"

By "out south" she meant the south—the black—side of town, a place regaled for its switchblade fights and wife beating, overreported in the *Herald* given the general lack of activity in other parts of town. His parents and others in their neighborhood took painfully circuitous routes around this area. Louis couldn't believe his sister's bravery—or foolishness.

"Who is he?" Louis asked when she was done with her explanation, feeling he was now in a position to ask.

Loretta turned away uncharacteristically. She was usually the one who could look straight at anything—a bright light, a dead cat, their mother's accusatory eyes.

"A friend."

"You mean boyfriend—"

"Well, he's not actually a boy." His sister looked at him. "You aren't going to tell on me, are you?"

Was he? He thought not, but he liked keeping her wondering. He liked all of this suddenly—life had been so boring before.

"I'll do anything you want, Louis, honest. Just don't tell them about him."

"But they already know something's going on—"

"They don't know who; they don't know his name. Who knows what they're liable to do? They might even call the police again . . ."

"You can't call the police for someone driving down the street," Louis retorted.

"You'd be surprised," Loretta said levelly.

"Yes," he said; he saw that he could be very much surprised.

"I won't say anything," he said, looking at his hands, small as biscuits, in his lap. He was vastly relieved that his sister was only linked to one person.

"Oh, Louis, thanks, thank you," Loretta said, reaching down to take one of his scrawny hands.

"But I'm afraid you're still gonna get in trouble," Louis continued. "Even if I don't say anything—"

"I'm already in trouble, Louis," his sister said, releasing his hand. "Can't you see that? I already am."

He could see it; he could suddenly see everything, as if he had been fitted with a strong set of corrective lenses.

He actually needed glasses, if you believed Harter and Harter Opticians, twin brothers in Gilbert, their mother's hometown, where he and Loretta were taken yearly for checkups. For someone who had wanted to escape a place as much as their mother, it seemed to Louis that she trusted Gilbert's doctors inordinately and was always returning there for one reason or another, besides visiting Louis's grandparents, who lived in a stately fashion, dispensing gifts and unequivocal love.

The Drs. Harter were like a comedy team. The sallow Dr. Joe Harter worked you up with jokes and eye charts, getting you ready for his more stolid, painful brother, Edmond, who inserted dilating drops and placed you behind equipment that you felt sure would cause pain.

These doctors were the ones who had fit Loretta with contact lenses at thirteen, freeing her once and for all from the thick glasses she had worn since she was a little girl. Louis couldn't help seeing this as a disservice, since his sister had been relatively safe behind the plastic frames that the doctors stocked in a wide variety of equally hideous shapes. Someone there favored pastel frames, pale as taffy, with flowers drilled into the sides. Loretta hadn't had a chance to be seductive in those—her eyes had swum behind them like tropical fish.

It was her misfortune that the doctors had bared her eyes, now covered only with a teardrop of plastic. Bare eyes were powerful—as powerful as bare breasts, Louis imagined—and ever since Loretta's had been revealed, she had been in trouble.

Louis had managed to talk his mother into waiting another year before he was placed under the Harters' correction himself. He was seeing enough already, possibly more than he could stand.

Now that he and Loretta had their old bond back, now that they were back to her spectacled days when they'd both been forgettable, Louis found it even more painful. Now he knew who would be mussing the hair Loretta teased each night, who would be smearing that glossy smile. He knew this better than his mother, who knew plenty, but didn't have a face to connect it with as Louis did, who didn't have the experience of that shining mouth.

The fights he witnessed were nearly unbearable. Whose side was he on?

When their mother said to Loretta, "You live in this house and have to abide by the rules"—her last and most common defense—wasn't she right, even though it was actually their father who financed their existence and should have been the one to lay down the law? In the navy, he had been submerged in a submarine for nearly a year and still had the quality of someone stunned by the surface. He seemed more comfortable with real wars than the skirmishes of family; whenever he spanked them, Louis found his aggrieved look more disturbing than the pain. Loretta had long ago stopped submitting to these punishments; when their father took off his belt now, it seemed laughable, or worse, connected to sex. Who could beat down this pink, towering creature?

But didn't Loretta also have a point, a variety of points, which she fanned out like a deck of cards? Wasn't she old enough to choose her own friends, of whatever hue or cut? Weren't you enough of a creature at seventeen to be accorded certain rights, such as privacy, for example?

Evidently not, for Louis witnessed their mother making furtive trips to Loretta's room during her absence; he once even came upon her in the laundry room studying her daughter's underpants (bought by her, yes, he knew this—he had even accompanied her to Jim's Pay & Save, where she'd bought twelve-packs for them both).

Louis felt like rising up in the middle of these shameful scenes and delivering a dramatic monologue. They would all be shocked by his new height (they had been too busy to notice, but he had grown in the last month), by his commanding stance.

"I can no longer abide living in this atmosphere," he would say, borrowing "abide" from his mother. "Both sides have their points, but they've been lost in petty technicalities. Because of my untenable position I've made plans to vacate the premises. Please forward my mail—" to where?

This is where his daydream became laughable, if it weren't laughable already. He had no mail and nowhere to go. He was still a pitiable five feet high with a breaking voice and a slouching gait. Everyone in the world towered over him, especially girls with their stacked heels. Why couldn't boys elevate themselves like this?

So he skulked around the edges of things, answering the phone on the first ring when he could, hoping to give this Luther person the experience of one neutral voice. Somehow he had become the umpire of his home, without anyone's knowing it, without anyone's caring.

But out in the world, out of the house, it was as if a third eye had been suddenly opened in the middle of his head. There were suddenly so many black people about—how had Louis failed to notice this?

He listened to their talk, standing at his locker, trying to remember where he belonged. Although he did well in school, it was only with considerable anxiety, and his worst nightmare was of forgetting where his next class was, of roaming the creaking halls of his school in a fog of amnesia, without a schedule to guide him. But the blacks in his school seemed to always know where they were—or were not—heading. Even when they skipped class, they did so with a certain assurance. Strong impulses seemed to tug them, while Louis followed the weak ropes of convention and duty.

He studied the faces of people with new intensity, the face of Mrs. Corrine Banks, his Spanish teacher, for example. Despite her rolled r's and jaunty accent, he saw that she had been a black woman all along. And stylish at that—much more stylish than the white women on their block, who moved in with the high color of brides and reappeared, weeks later it seemed to Louis, as matrons, slovenly in housecoats, their hair raked back from their faces so they could see dirt, or whatever it was they sought so intently at their feet. Despite great odds and a certain age, Mrs. Banks continued to lacquer her nails so they gleamed like jewelry at the end of her hands; she continued to powder a smooth brown countenance set with lively eyes that snapped with knowledge of dipthongs—and who knew what else.

The world was suddenly thick with all Louis had never noticed: Lateshas and Adremmas, who jumped double dutch after class; the ancient janitor, Mr. Morris, and his motley maintenance gang, who appeared on the last page of the yearbook, identified only by their mops. Watching them, Louis now discerned grace in the slosh of their rags.

He was aware that he was probably overdoing all

this—that perhaps he was seeing more than there was. This seemed to be another trait of his family, perhaps the best one; they all sometimes took things too far. But he was happy with this expanded view for the moment, this feeling of largesse that he felt for almost everyone who fell under his gaze. It was the flip side of the point of view he'd had for so long, when everything was miserly and wan. For a few months at least, the world seemed to open up its arms to him with a sigh.

Louis yearned to share all this with Loretta, but he could only get to her late at night when she returned home pale and spent. The feelings he had, which she must share, had not done her much good if her looks were any sign. Something seemed to be eating away at her. Her face was thinner (this gave him personal hope that his own head might grow); her eyes, either from smudged makeup or deep emotion, looked gaunt. At least she talked to him now; he was glad of that. But Loretta's stories of tight scrapes and missed connections on streets that sounded out of a recipe—Sugar Street, Water Street, Milk—made him sleepless afterward; he was excited and afraid for her at the same time.

And more was going on than her intrigues on Sugar Street, where she'd informed him Luther lived with his mother, Annie. People had begun talking about her in earnest. Louis didn't tell her about the phone calls he intercepted: *Your sister's a nigger lover; How does it feel to be related to a whore?*

He recognized these voices—the same boys who had

called Loretta with far different intent several months ago. He said their names, Darrell Lutes, Beau Brown, when his mother asked him. This served some purpose; she was relieved that white boys were still calling.

But everything else was going wrong: Loretta's grades had plummeted, as if she'd lost her brains along with her heart. Their mother was called in for an algebra conference with the notorious, big-hipped Mrs. Cloris Spalding, who was glad to report that Loretta asked for a pass at the beginning of the class and spent whole periods in the hall. This was true—Loretta didn't deny it—she didn't even care about defending herself now.

"What's the point of algebra?" she asked Louis, as if he should know. Her vulnerability worried him. She seemed open to not only love but viruses; she caught colds now nearly every month.

And en masse, his family lost its appetite. No one wanted his mother's meals anymore. Her meat loaf sat in brown squares on brown plates, like a punishment.

"Fine," she said, "I'll just stop cooking. I've got better things to do," making Louis flush with unhappiness, because he wasn't sure this was true.

Turning from a boy into a man was hard enough, but Louis saw it might be even harder to leave the realm of girls. Being desired took an awful toll; even Loretta seemed to be tiring of it. He felt she was relieved to take out her contacts and put on her thick pink glasses and stained chenille robe. He felt honored when she sat down in front of him like this, as if finally presenting her plain and guileless self for his fearful inspection.

"Be careful," he wanted to say to her these nights. He had to keep himself from taking her by the elbow and propelling her somewhere out of harm's way.

All Louis's worrying was in vain, because this scene ended abruptly, as if it were an act in a play. Louis had only seen a few plays himself, painful high school productions, where everything was clear as soon as the characters came on stage—who would love whom and when; the drama department at Union High School was notoriously weak.

But he would not have foreseen this particular ending. It was not Loretta who had hinted at it, but his mother.

"Your sister's going away to school," she told him the week before Easter. They were both in the kitchen swallowing—he a hard-boiled egg, she a piece of toast. The great gold yolk felt lodged in his throat, and he had to contract it several times before he could ask, "Where?"

"Cincinnati."

"When?"

"Next week."

"Why?"

"Because she has to," his mother said.

This was a Saturday night, or he would have gone upstairs to talk to Loretta. He went up anyway and sat on her striped bedspread and breathed in her air. A pink shoe that she had tried on and then discarded lay on its side on the rug. He picked it up by its great spike and saw how scuffed it was, how the heel, tiny as a dime, was worn away.

"I can't talk," she said two nights in a row when he went up to her at midnight, and after that he couldn't keep himself from falling asleep before she arrived. He fell into a deep pit of sleep where couples twisted and kissed deeply from the depths of their mouths. When he woke, doors had been closed all over the house; his parents' faces looked like oak.

There was extra band practice that week for a concert that weekend, and he was distracted by the complicated rhythms of a Latin tune in which he had a featured part. At one point, all the other music stopped and he had to blow away on his own. There was no getting around this—it was right there on the score—unless he feigned sickness, and, unlike his sister, he didn't know how.

But he was relieved when his mother told him on Wednesday that they were taking Loretta away that weekend and wouldn't be able to come to his concert. He drank Coke that night and watched television in order to stay awake. Loretta arrived home at 11:15 in the middle of the sports report—the Union basketball team had lost again, this time out of town. She peeked into the family room, where their father was stretched out snoring; their mother had long since retreated to her room. Then she focused on Louis, who stood up, as if a zombie, and followed her up the stairs.

He waited for her to speak, but she began undoing

herself instead—taking hoops out of the holes in her ears, kicking off shoes, unzipping her waistband, which looked tight. Louis was relieved to see this; she must be eating, at least.

Watching her, he wondered if she were going to undress right there in front of him. He would have been glad to view his sister's body once and for all, to see what all this life had done to her, whether she was smoothed by it or sharpened. He bet on smoothed—he imagined her eroded away from so much love and trouble, from being turned over and over by warm hands in the dark. But she went into the bathroom at the last moment, so he never knew for sure.

Louis moved to her tiny window and looked out at the flat plot of crabgrass next door. Their neighbors on this side were a barbarous family who kept their female dog trapped on a mangled length of rusty chain attached to the back porch. She was there now, she was always there, in a brown curl, her black snoot in the dirt. In the past Loretta had poured water in her bone-dry bowl each morning. But it had been a long while since Louis had seen her do this, and the dog's forgotten thirst rose up all at once in his throat.

Loretta emerged from the bathroom smelling of mint and sat down on her bed. She sat down on it like a dog herself, as if she had a tail to contend with.

"Come here," she said, and Louis turned away from the window and joined her in one movement; he didn't even feel his feet on the floor.

They had shared this room once, divided by a peg-

board partition upon which hung jaunty reminders of
their sex—ballcaps and pennants on Louis's side, floral
arrangements on Loretta's. But they still shared this one
closet, hung with two pale slabs of wood, in whose
grain odd shapes could be discerned. Loretta had always
seen a weeping woman with a long neck, her hair falling
forward over her eyes. Louis had seen zebras until Loretta pointed the woman out—now he saw her also.
They both looked at the woman as Loretta took his hand
and placed it across her stomach. It wasn't her heart she
was driving at, although he could feel it thudding dis-
tantly, above and to the left. Or maybe it was her heart
she was thinking of, but she was telling him something
else.

Something happened to Louis that spring. For one
thing he grew, two and a half inches in four months,
and gained eight pounds. It was as if some impediment
had been removed from somewhere above him, and
when he ate potatoes or broccoli they stayed with him.
He felt the flank of the cow he chewed adhere to his
legs; leafy vegetables moved straight to his hair.

And he'd done so well on his solo that he received
special mention on his report card and was asked if he
would mind doing it again in the fall.

"No," he said, surprising himself as much as he'd
been surprised during the concert. He found he liked
the hot spotlight, the moment when he was called upon
to make his own particular noise.

And he made a friend, two friends really, since they

came together, as if in a packaged set. They were a direct result of the concert, two brainy boys, one a drum player, the other first clarinet. Louis had impressed them with his competence, and they invited him to form a trio with them. Even the word *trio* pleased Louis, suggesting some snug and lucky person in the middle, and he immediately accepted.

And as if this weren't enough, there was a girl named Carolyn who liked him, who even sent him an Easter card (he hadn't known there were cards for such occasions) and used the pretense of being in his math class to call him at night. He knew it was a pretense because he had sat behind her long enough to know she was smart, perhaps even smarter than he was. But he let the pretense stand—he saw you had to do this—that girls often performed certain acts of diminishment in order to connect with boys and men.

He was least confident of this last piece of luck. Besides being smart, Carolyn was so pretty, with her length of beige hair and perfect mouth, that he kept expecting her to recant, to phone him one evening (for she called him most evenings, right after dinner; she was brave, after all) and say, "I've just come from Harter and Harter Opticians and had my vision adjusted, and I see I've been mistaken about you all along."

But this didn't happen, and anyway, he thought, the rest was nearly enough. Some warm mornings he went out to shoot baskets on the wet lawn, just to note how much easier it was with his height. He couldn't get enough of it, putting the ball effortlessly through the hoop time and time again. One morning he actually saw his mother watching from the kitchen window and caught that most foreign of displays in their household of late—an impromptu smile.

His parents went to Cincinnati once a month, but didn't ask him to accompany them, and he was just as glad. He had things to do now, his own things, and the thought of his sister, who was going on to college from her so-called girl's school, caused a raw ache in his chest.

Her room had been closed up since her departure, as if in memorial to who she once was. Someone—their mother, he supposed—had gathered up relics of those last months, the *Ebony* magazines and short skirts, and put them away, he didn't know where.

Along with much else, Carolyn had introduced him to the world of greeting cards, with their vague but adequate messages, and Louis sent one to Loretta whenever he had a chance. "It's sure warm here," he wrote across the bottom, or "Hope you're all right." These messages were as empty as the party line calls he'd once listened in to, but his pen stopped after three or four words.

He sometimes wondered if he were being heartless by not picking up the phone and calling the number he knew his parents had, if he simply asked. But it was as if some wound had just healed over with a membrane of skin, and he was the only one who could tend it. This layer was so new that it often threatened to crack. Carolyn particularly challenged it, and the night of their first so-called date—a mere walk to the Kingburger a few days after Loretta's departure—he thought it might break again for good.

There was nothing wrong with this night that Louis could find, though out of habit, he tried. The feelings he'd had earlier in the year were gone now: Union had reverted back to its plain self. But even with its cracked sidewalks and overcast weekends, it didn't seem so bad.

Carolyn wore a blue dress and even smelled blue, as if she had rolled in indigo flowers. She had not only orchestrated this dinner, but took his hand during their walk. She evidently could take care of it all. As they approached the restaurant, Louis's mind was filled with so much pleasure—he could already taste what he planned to eat, a Kingburger and fries, his favorite meal—that it took him a moment to register who was sitting in the drive-in section as he and Carolyn moved across the lot.

Carolyn was talking about math again—he hoped she would shortly drop this nonsense—when he caught sight of Luther's head, not alone of course; that would have been too much. Luther caught his gaze, as if he'd thrown a ball to him, and Louis stopped a moment in his tracks.

"What's wrong?" Carolyn asked, clamping on to his hand.

"Just a minute. I'll be right back." He let go of her—this was difficult, she had so thoroughly entwined them—and walked over to the red car. In the hot beam of the Kingburger's spotlights, it didn't look so sumptuous; there was a rust spot and a long dent that he hadn't noticed before. But it still had music in it; a low trill floated out as he approached the driver's side and Luther climbed out, leaving a chewing woman, brown and pretty, inside.

"Hey, little brother," Luther said, extending his hand, and Louis, feeling manly with this gesture under Carolyn's watchful eye, extended his own and shook, the first real shake of his life.

But he didn't know what to say after this, and as the silence ticked away, accompanied by that music, he felt that old ache again. Luther took his elbow and veered him a few steps away from the car.

"She's gone," Louis suddenly blurted out, unable to stand the buildup. He made himself look up at Luther; even with two and a half new inches, he still had to look up. "She told everyone it's a girl's school, but no one believes her. We had to get our number changed—people were calling in the middle of the night, waking us up." He had to keep himself from saying what he had planned to say for weeks now, if he ever got Luther on the phone: Have mercy! he wanted to cry out, like the Dixie Hummingbirds. Have mercy on us!

Luther looked at him, at his eyes, Louis thought, and altered his mouth. "Ah, man," he sighed, rubbing his hair, which held the imprint of some hat he'd taken off. Then he turned his gaze back toward the car, and the moment was gone.

They shook hands again, and Louis pivoted away, walking blindly toward the spot of swimming blue waiting for him on the asphalt. It was all he could make out at the moment, and he was just as glad.

PART TWO

CHAPTER 1

THE SUMMER BEFORE Mrs. Holmes's death, Junior Johnson had disowned his daughter, Elaine, knowing that such a thing wasn't really possible. But his background in literature, especially a spell of long Russian novels, had given him a taste for the large gesture, and he didn't seem to be able to keep himself, in times of crisis, from being melodramatic.

Elaine had committed only one act that he disapproved of—marrying a local boy named Luther Biggs who was far below her potential—but it was a tragic act as Junior saw it, one that negated years of other acts, performed by him, that would ensure her eventual success. He had steered her into honors clubs and accelerated math; he'd ordered her special leather volumes, coveted by the Union public library.

"She was fit for Harvard!" he cried.

His wife, Helene, was suspicious of his sanctimoniousness; toward the end she had grown suspicious of everything, as if a blindfold had been torn from her eyes.

73

"This has to do with you, not Elaine," she told him after he barred their daughter from the house. "Just because you're a failure, doesn't mean she can't be too."

It had become clear by this point that Helene also saw herself as a failure, and mostly due to him. She'd come into her own marriage with high prospects; this was why Junior had picked her—a flair for debate, a flair for fashion and speaking her mind—and for many months after their wedding, she had appeared at their dinner table dressed and primed for more than the burned meal she'd managed to scrape together. She hated meat—Junior's dietary mainstay—and brought it to the table as mangled as if she'd tussled with it in a fight.

"It's a roast," she said combatively when Junior asked of the dish's derivation. "A chunk of flesh torn from a cow. Isn't that what you like?"

Junior saw that admiration and matrimony did not necessarily go together; that what he had been drawn to in Helene had no space in their limited life. Gradually, she began to leave off her jeweled earrings when he came in each evening; her private research, which she'd insisted on space for when they married, remained enigmatic, then vanished. Junior had few friends and Helene lost hers to the public sector—women who had walked off on high heels toward large places: Cleveland, Chicago, Detroit. And how many debates could she win— and how fruitfully—with a melancholy mortician who also happened to be her husband?

Junior had always known that he wanted a daughter. Being in the funeral business as long as he had, he felt there were already plenty of men. He had yet to see a wound inflicted by a woman; he had never seen a female fight back with anything more than the palm of her hand.

Even his own energy, loud and broad, baffled and dismayed him, and he'd observed with envy the quiet power of his wife before marriage leached it away.

Twins and males ran on Helene's side of the family, and they were both convinced up till the end of her pregnancy that she would have two of something, probably boys. She had been big enough for triplets, as far as Junior was concerned, but it had only been Elaine, unfolding herself like a colt, ass first, legs next, brown and wet and warm.

It was not clear what Helene had hoped for; she had announced, "I'm pregnant," in the same flat way as she had said throughout their marriage, "I'm bored."

She'd always remained apart, even when her sisters and their children came to visit, robust women with simple pleasures and double prams. Her sisters were not like Helene; they did not even look like her. She had taken the lean planed face of some ancestor now long vanished. Her solemnity was absent in both of her siblings, who wore pastels and had passions for bedrest and chocolate and sex. Helene never slept much, even when she was pregnant; even then Junior felt that a part of her was on the lookout for some danger, and that it might be in him. In fact, she didn't do many of the things other women did naturally. She was leery of stoves and wouldn't wear high heels because she already towered over most women and some men and had confided to Junior during their brief courtship, "You can't get away fast if you wear them."

Junior had half expected her to flee him then and continued to expect it in some part of himself until the mounting years fooled him into believing that she was his, for good.

She'd watched Junior thrill over their daughter with an odd look, part bemusement, part something unnamed. Over the years, he had been the one who pressed for frilly clothes, the overabundance of toys, the one who played airplane to get Elaine to eat her vegetables, cooked by Helene into a grasslike mulch. Even when Elaine was a newborn, Helene rarely held her, and then as if she were a loaf of bread.

"You love her, don't you?" Junior had asked once in alarm when Elaine was still little, and Helene had looked up at him, and said, "She's me. Again."

But Junior didn't think so. He thought she was him and his magnificent mother in the orange urn in his living room; he thought she was all the wondrous, stalwart women stretched back in his family, storyless.

"Me and Mommy love you so much," he said at night to his daughter, in a voice intended for his wife. Helene did not encourage—or even discourage—the intimacy that he insisted prevail, presenting her cheek to her daughter each evening impassively, as if for an injection.

Junior was the one who had plaited Elaine's heavy hair, which Helene only brushed out in a utilitarian fashion to keep it from her eyes.

"Being pretty won't help her," she told Junior when he pushed for bows and braids and partings other than the center.

"She's not going to just be pretty," he told her. "She's going to be smart."

But Helene had turned away from this, as she did all of his answers; she had made it clear that there would never be another child.

"Let Elaine be," she said to him over the years. "She comes from two fools. What do you expect?"

It was comments like this that allowed Junior to feel relief when she vacated the premises herself, a month after their daughter. He had felt illuminated by his faults during those last months of marriage; he moved through the rooms aglow with his own peevishness. But Helene had been far easier to lose than Elaine, whose delicate, deerlike quality had made her a graceful presence in the house. At least someone wasn't done yet, Junior thought when she was around. The thought of her possibilities, when he came upon her reading or doing something as simply physical as climbing a flight of steps, buoyed and inspired him. He and Helene seemed boiled down to their inert and bitter essence, while Elaine was all ephemeral, ungathered; imagining her convergence took up much of his time.

But Helene had not been so boiled down after all. Before she left, she went back to school to enter the realm of accounting and procured, from some unknown source, sheer white blouses that suggested the round breasts she now kept hidden from him. He came upon her pulling her long legs into panty hose of a dark and delicate pattern, encasing her trunk in sleek, tailored sheaths.

He saw that you never knew what was in people, or when it might arise; that traits, long buried, might break out at any time, like a virus.

From all accounts, his jewel-like daughter had become docilely, hugely pregnant, flipping the switch of her mind to off. After mastering Latin, she had settled for an attic bedroom, badly ventilated, and the long, dark arms of a young man who would probably never vote.

Junior could barely think of his daughter's married life, even though it was occurring at every moment he existed only a few miles away in an adjacent part of town. He could look at his dead mother's ashes and his own divorce decree more easily than he could contemplate Elaine, National Honor Society member and homecoming queen, boiling Minute Rice, bending down to the linoleum with a rag.

"Daddy!" she had implored in the middle of his last tirade, when he had stood on his own front steps and railed at Luther Biggs, who slumped in his red Mustang. And even after two years, it was this plain word, in her voice, that woke him most nights.

Elaine Johnson Biggs nursed her son, Roman, past two, much longer than was recommended. She was good at it, without textbooks or instructors, and liked the deep contraction in her uterus when her boy closed lips like a mandarin orange around her breast. It was the same ache that had preceded her coupling with her husband, Luther Biggs, but he had not touched it; he had only shoved it deeper, until now she sometimes felt the ache way up, in her chest.

Annie Biggs, Luther's mother, warned her that she was nursing Roman too long. "Boys have a hard enough time breaking from their mamas. He'll be following you around the rest of his life."

But she didn't say this with much gusto, given the facts of her own life. She had not nursed Luther at all, yet here he was, living in her upstairs bedroom with a wife and child in tow.

Elaine knew she had furthered the confusion of this house on Sugar Street by implanting herself as a dependent; it was not a place that needed another body—already there weren't enough washcloths and pillow slips and juice glasses to go around.

She thought these things; then she lifted her son to her breast and she stopped thinking at all. Roman had a saucer face and a sparse lawn of hair on top of his head. He looked like a Buddha and Luther actually grimaced the first time he saw him, saying, "You sure he's ours?"

"Yes," Elaine had murmured, waiting for more, but that had been all.

Elaine was still amazed that she and Luther had conspired to create anything as tangible as a baby. You would have thought that Luther would have to be off cigarettes and the beer he drank in pints throughout the summer; you would have thought the white girl he'd made pregnant would have to be gone more than a few months.

But none of that had been required, only a long, overcast summer weekend on a bed with sprung springs. No soft music or words of love, just a man down on Sugar Street vainly trying to start the engine of his Coupe de Ville.

Elaine only saw later, when it was over, what had been wrong with the scene: Luther had left his sneakers on throughout their lovemaking—he had picked her up on his way from playing basketball; Elaine's bra was around her neck and there was blood, maroon as choir robes, on his leg and lip and arm. They looked like they had been in an accident.

Luther hadn't thought it was funny when she told him this. She'd been learning about him, minute by minute, in that odd laboratory, the bed.

"There wasn't any accident about it. You gonna deny now that you wanted it too?"

But Elaine had stood up in the interim and could barely balance herself on the balls of her feet. She hadn't been about to deny anything.

The other night, after Luther had made love to her in the same driven fashion as that first time, he said, "I'm disappointing you," and from her inert position, Elaine thought, That's a rhetorical remark.

And then her mind wandered to a class she had once

taken in communications, and that took her further back to a paper she had written on irony, until she forgot Luther had spoken at all. When he finally dislodged himself in the darkness, she was startled; he looked like a stranger. Close up, his handsomeness broke down, like the dotted faces of cartoons.

She continued to expect some linear movement from her husband, but she couldn't bring herself to say what it was. He had yet to bring home a real paycheck, and Elaine had no clear idea what they were living on. Pregnancy, then motherhood, had dwindled her reserves of wit and analysis; she felt moronic, but peaceful. Her body would take care of things where her mind had failed her—it knew what it was doing better than she did. And her body seemed enough for her husband and son, who did not appear to mind her monosyllabic talk. They both came to her—Roman with his sucking lips, Luther with his bulging trousers—like sleepwalkers. But some other part of her brain kicked in some nights as she was being fed on or filled up, speaking down to her first in the tones of her father, then her mother, saying, "This isn't enough."

Elaine still couldn't accept that her parents had separated after twenty years of marriage. She'd received a note from Helene telling her so, but she still couldn't believe it. Her parents remained frozen in the scene where she had last left them—Junior crying out on the front porch, Helene peering from behind lace. She couldn't dislodge them from these positions, in spite of the postmark on her mother's letter, somewhere in Illinois, where she claimed to have a friend and a job and a phone. The number was there for Elaine to call—ten digits—but she did not do so, just as she had successfully avoided the section of town where Junior now lived alone. To reconnect with either of her parents would require breaking her current position and taking another look at herself.

Distance was in the mind, as was time; Elaine knew enough physics—and now life—to understand that. When Junior had said, "The moment you married Biggs, you quit being my daughter," something had stopped in Elaine, like a clock, and a new one had begun ticking when she had backed down the fieldstone steps of her house and folded herself into Luther's car. Luther would not leave her, she had thought then, not with an embryo curled like a snail inside. It was that added weight, like a small round stone in her pelvis, that had made her marriage seem authentic. And so she had put her pink birth control pills in her half of the underwear drawer that once housed Annie's linen, clear, at least for the moment, what she had to continue to do.

Luther Biggs was getting himself together. This was what he said, in explanation of himself, when anyone asked. He had dozens of ideas when he was in the relative safety of his mother's bedroom—scenes where he starred as a businessman in fine wool suits, telling secretaries what letters to write, what other secretaries to call. At other times he saw himself overseeing white work crews, initialing their time cards, fixing things with his hands. Some nights he wrote down what he was good at, and the list was long. But then he would come downstairs to find his wife, fresh from the honor roll, hunched over a can of Delmonte green beans. Or he would walk into an office for an interview and catch the no in the eyes of white receptionists, even before he'd filled out the forms.

"We'll get back to you, Mr. Biggs," they said, after he answered their questions, but Annie's phone only rang at night, and then with wrong numbers or his older sister, Netty, wanting to borrow something, usually milk, from her apartment in the house next door.

Luther could not believe that in the not-so-distant past he had actually slept with the daughters of such women, that at a variety of times, in a variety of situations, he'd let white girls wrap their pale legs around his back. He thought of his hands in their dense, straight hair and wondered why he hadn't grabbed on and pulled it out. He'd had so many, right under him—he could've done whatever he wanted. But he had only looked Loretta in the face and she was the one who had become pregnant; it was Loretta who had finally snagged something inside him, like a nail. Why had she picked him from the dim herds roaming the halls of Union High School? Why had she ever let herself be picked by him? What should have been just another anonymous toss in bed had turned substantial with her pregnancy. It made her stand out from all the other girls he'd known before, solid as marble. He tried to imagine their daughter, now adopted, celebrating her birthday in some white couple's home, playing in the center of a fertilized lawn. What box did they check when they filled out forms for her? he wondered. Without him or Loretta, how had they ever come up with a name? What DNA of his was buried inside her? He wanted to see his daughter's wiring at least, even if he never saw the rest of her.

Luther let his mother and wife think he was out looking for work each day, but after months of dead ends, he went to Linwood Center and shot basketballs instead. It took him back to those hot afternoons of his middle childhood, before things had become hard, for good. Then he'd had a sack lunch and his gym bag and the whole warm day until dusk, when he walked back home and opened the door to the smell of stewing chicken and Annie saying, "Give me those socks out of your gym bag," then dropping them into a soup of Tide.

He saw that men really needed their mothers later, after they'd had a whiff of the bitterness of the world and its meager comforts. He felt sure that no matter how old they were, he and Elaine could never duplicate the warmth that Annie had preserved here—in the seasoned couch, where endless people had sunk down throughout the years, in the artery of carpet, worn with trails of going to the bathroom again, getting a chicken wing again, of heading out the battered front door, to once again try. Even the phone receiver was fragrant with ear wax and hair oil; no one had ever cleaned it as far as Luther knew, and he liked to think of what had been heard from it and said.

When Annie was gone, Luther was sure this house would go too, that it would collapse at her mere absence, just as it stood only under her plain care. It was her house, and when he wanted to think of the most painful thing he could imagine, it was walking through that wide door frame and calling out, "Mama!" and not having her answering voice ring out, "In here."

Her room especially could never be cleared of her, the walls layered with the shifting tastes of her life—the pink-picked florals of her early years, the splashier yellows of her ripeness, the Colonial ladies and plain blue sky shades of her middle years and now her last ones. Her smell, a scent that adhered to her after showers, an odor that Luther picked up on clothes long dry-cleaned and packed with mothballs, seemed to originate here, in the folds of her quilted bed. It was the original odor of his life, and leaving it, and this house, often seemed more than he could manage.

He had no smell of his own as far as he could tell, and Elaine's slightly alkaline scent was easily masked by whatever lotion she spread over herself. Compared to Annie, he and Elaine seemed without weight or consequence, minor characters moving on the surface of the visible world. But Annie had dug in and lived deep, a life so rich and interior that it gave off a smell.

"How'd your day go, baby?" she asked every evening when he returned, while Elaine looked on in silence; perhaps she knew where he went. Her future was in his hands now, and he wondered if they were big enough to hold her. It reminded him of a song from Sunday school when he'd gone to the Baptist church as a child, "He's Got the Whole World in His Hands."

Some nights he sat and stared at his, black and double-jointed. Elaine liked him to touch her with them, more than she liked anything else. But he only used them with her as tools, as preliminary instruments. All he really wanted to do at night, when Annie and the baby were asleep and he was still unemployed, was sink into his wife with the base of his body, delve into the tender center of her where she enfolded him in spite of herself.

CHAPTER 2

ANNIE BIGGS HAULED herself out of bed each morning; that's how it felt, as if she were pulling up her body like a bag of coal. Life was weight, and hers had finally descended on her in the last year, at 57, when she decided she was old. It was her spirit that told her this more than her body, which had ached and vexed her since her forties. But no one knew what she really felt inside the frame of herself, because she didn't believe in complaint.

When Luther asked, "How you feelin', Mama?" he required a particular kind of answer of her and she gave it automatically, "Fine, baby," year after year.

Her friends and neighbors assumed she was happy with so much life in her house—with her son and his wife and child. And it wasn't that she minded their presence or cared whether Elaine burned up every pot in her house, or that her grandson woke her with his staccato footsteps before she was ready to be back in the world again.

But Luther was holding on here too long for his own

good, and she didn't know what would become of him.
She was alarmed to find him collapsed in the chair of
her living room in the exact same position as when he
was in high school. She couldn't see what growing older
had done for him. There were new things in his face
some mornings, but she was afraid they weren't self-
reliance and fortitude—the things she hoped for. And
Elaine wore nothing on her face now but the flat sheen
of the dependent. The face Annie had glimpsed the first
weeks she had met her was now as gone as if she'd hung
it in the closet along with the fancy clothes of her former
life. The happiest creature here was the baby, Roman,
who was fed and loved and warm, for the moment
oblivious.

To distract herself, Annie daydreamed about what
she would do if she ever won fifty thousand dollars on
"Jeopardy," which she watched nonstop on various
channels, from eleven to two each day. First, she'd fix
her front porch, which was threatening to fall off any
year now, in one rotted mass. Then she'd do her teeth,
chipped and golden with time and neglect. She wasn't
sure what the dentist would make of them. The last time
she'd gone, the white girl who was the assistant had
drawn back, as if in horror, when Annie opened her
mouth.

"Could you tell me your dental regime?" she asked,
grabbing a clipboard and pen, and Annie had replied,
"I brush with salt."

The girl had then disappeared for so long that Annie
eventually stood up and left with her napkin still

clamped on. She was sure that if she had money, they'd never treat her like that.

These two items were both important entrances— her front porch supported her family and visitors, introducing them to her world, and her mouth did the same. She had always been ashamed of her teeth, even when she was a girl. She'd had an overbite then, but it had shifted over the years.

"Your mouth changes every day," a dentist had once told her, in her twenties. She thought them all especially wise and would go to them frequently if she had the funds.

But after fixing these two items, she'd spend the rest of the money on everyone else. She'd put a downpayment on a house for Luther and finance his starting a business. Since he claimed he couldn't work for other people, she wanted to help him find a way to work for himself. And she wanted him to know how it felt to own a circle of lawn in which you could do whatever you wanted—where you could sing out loud or burn trash or grow sunflowers. She would give him seeds from her own backyard and show him how to plant them, if he'd stand still long enough. And she wanted to buy her daughter, Netty, a new wardrobe so that she could throw out the ratty fake fur coat she had worn since she was in high school, a coat that strained at the seams every time she tried to button it, accentuating how much she had grown in certain physical ways.

And for all her grandchildren, she wanted to set up a savings for college. The idea of her offspring laden

89

with books, excelling in some future she would not live to see, thrilled her. Then, with what money was left, she would hire a private detective to find Loretta and her daughter. Annie did not think she could die well until she had laid eyes on this, her unknown granddaughter, at least in a photograph, at least for a moment.

Of course, she preferred to see her in the flesh, for at least an hour. Then she could tell her how she and her mother had been during that strange autumn of 1969.

Annie hadn't been able to look at Loretta too closely when Luther first brought her; her silhouette reminded her of a rangy redhead her husband, Horace, had gone around with for a time. By that point, their marriage was already in tatters: Horace had been laid off from the Ford plant and Annie'd been forced to clean houses on the other side of town. Waiting for the bus in the morning, she'd watch him cruise by with this woman in a cloud of radio song.

"There goes Horace," she'd say, before the other women she stood with could comment.

This particular woman lasted only a season—an autumn of her floral cologne in their foyer, paper notes stuck in the windshield of her husband's car—but these vivid promenades formed Horace's reputation around town.

That woman's name was Doris, and she had been in her forties with a stained, toothsome smile. She was of a certain category of white woman Annie was well aware of at the time; it was only here—on the south side of Union—that anyone still treated her as special.

But this Loretta was different. Seen from a window,

she looked stylish, even seductive, but up close you could see something starved. More than a man or an audience, she seemed to yearn for another home for herself. She sat at their table, eating salt pork and chitlins, asking Annie one question after the next. How flattering Annie found this—just to be asked. She put her elbows on the table and forgot herself, talking on while Luther sighed.

Annie knew that the young needed things from their elders, but wasn't this what your family was for? Why was this girl on the other side of the tracks, hungry for stories; her family must have had plenty of their own. And why the first night they met did Annie tell her one tale after another, culminating with the story of a Jewish woman in their old neighborhood named Mrs. Koo, who had become obsessed with returning to Germany right before the war, and finally made it back just in time to be taken off to the camps.

"She dreamed about going back there, like you would about Tahiti or something," she told Loretta. "I could never get over that. She wanted to go back."

Luther fidgeted—even as a boy he hated hearing sad stories. He averted his head at the first shift in fortune, as if his ear couldn't tolerate it.

"We'd better go," he said when she finished. "I've gotta get Loretta home."

They were at the dining room table, and it took a beat or two before Annie remembered who they were.

"It is late," she said, smoothing a placemat. She felt embarrassed, like a girl who'd revealed too much.

She adjusted herself to be more aloof, but the next

time Luther brought Loretta, he put on his jacket after only an hour.

"You're leaving her with me?"

"She says she wants me to. She doesn't like going out to bars."

"Why don't you take her home, then?"

Luther stood behind her; she could feel his breath on her neck. Since Horace had left them, he'd tried bringing home bachelors and widowers; he'd tried many things to please and distract her, contending she was lonelier than she thought.

"She doesn't want to go home, but I'll take her if you want."

Annie turned around and saw her house, as if a stranger, for the first time. What did this white girl want in her hot, jumbled rooms, dense with the fragrance of pork?

"No, leave her," she said.

When Luther returned later, he looked in the window and saw Annie and Loretta braiding a length of yarn, working toward each other, their heads bent under the kitchen light. On the table was the tattered maroon photograph album that contained Annie's girlhood and a tin of cornbread, half gone. At the creak of his step, Loretta looked up blindly at the black window, and something dipped in Luther's chest. Maybe this had been a mistake, after all.

"Who is *that?*" his sister, Netty, whispered to him a while later, coming up out of the dark world to the porch swing where Luther remained, smoking his third cigarette.

He shrugged in the darkness.

"You brought home a *white* girl?"

"No, she just wandered in."

Luther wished that this scene would end, just as it was, without further action on his part, that after doing whatever she was doing with his mother, this girl would dematerialize in front of their eyes. She was more trouble than he had bargained for, and he tried to avoid trouble in love. He had picked Loretta as he had picked all girls—as a challenge, just to see if he could do it. He did not like it when she looked at him so closely or gripped his hand. He did not like how she fathomed his whereabouts in the complex migration of high school, appearing like a stoic apparition at locations he seemed drawn to by magnetism.

He had meant to have her once, twice at the most, and then only physically, yet here she was, smack in the middle of his home.

"I feel like I shouldn't even go in there," Nettie said now, hovering at the door.

"Go on," Luther said, standing up. "It's my problem. I'll have to take care of it."

He had taken care of it, all right; he'd gone right ahead and impregnated her; it might even have been the next night.

They had been in his bedroom, separated from the hallway by a shower curtain, and using the rubbers that were in his dresser drawer would have made him hesitate long enough to ruin the forward thrust of his passion.

What should he have done? Loretta was there, and Annie was next door playing gin, and they were full of a dinner so resplendent with gravy and butter that Luther felt leaden with desire.

This is the last time, he told himself, just as he did when he lit a cigarette, as he lowered himself into her arms.

He was becoming aware of her in a fashion that was far deeper than necessary. He found himself worrying after he dropped her off at the corner of her street. Did her parents confront her? How much did she have to lie?

And something about her looked smeared when he saw her in school now. She seemed disoriented behind her rosy face, which was irritated by his beard, he realized.

Why continue with this? he asked himself. Why let Annie become accustomed to her company? Why let his body? But when Loretta moved close enough, he fell into her force field, as if it were a chamber. So he closed his eyes to the hard facts of the world. One more time.

That night Luther discovered it was not so much sex but sleeping with someone that was the most intimate act of all. When Loretta drifted off beside him, he studied the globe of her head. Who was this person? At times, up close like this, she seemed as alien as someone from another planet. But then her foot nestled next to his leg and she made a small snarling snore, and he felt an animal kinship that both moved and frightened him. There was something heartbreaking about her in repose, the white clenched fist by her face on the pillow, as if she were holding on to something dear. He kept meaning to get up and through his movements wake her, but he drifted off himself. The next thing he knew there was a light in the hall and the silhouette of his mother in the doorway, the front of her blackened out. She didn't say anything; they simply blinked at each other in the darkness, like two creatures who need a moment to establish who they are.

Luther ate the first eggroll of his life at Wong's Chinese Palace on the night, several months later, when Loretta told him she was being sent to a home for unwed mothers.

"I'll come see you," he said when their food arrived.

"No, you can't," Loretta said. "It's not allowed."

"What do you mean, it's not allowed. Is it a prison or something?"

Loretta splayed open her eggroll and studied the ingredients, as if for a quiz.

"It's a religious home, Luther. They're strict."

"You mean they don't like blacks."

Loretta shrugged. "I don't know. I guess they don't like anyone. Especially the boys who did it."

Luther flinched. She made him sound as if he were a murderer. He didn't like her use of *it*. "So you're being punished on top of everything else."

Loretta shrugged again and that was his answer: Yes, she was. Yes, she thought she deserved it.

Luther bit into his eggroll and a rivulet of grease seeped out of his mouth. He chewed the strange, crisp wad and studied Loretta as he had never studied her before; she hadn't said how much time they had left. Annie had known she was pregnant for a while now, but he still couldn't see it.

"I'd marry you," he said after a moment, when his mouth was clear again.

Loretta raised her glass of water to her lips and looked up at him over it, and there she was in that look, the person he had senselessly loved for four whole months, practically a record. He watched her long neck as it took down the liquid and it was the last best moment they had.

The following ones were not so good, and Luther tried not to remember them. After dinner Loretta had retreated into a cool, almost holy shell, where she couldn't be reached.

"Annie'll take the baby if you can't handle it."

"That would be the same as my keeping it," Loretta said.

"No, it's not. And so what? It's not just your precious future we're talking about here. What about mine? What about the baby?"

"I am thinking about the baby," Loretta said softly.

"Oh, I see. And you don't think my kind of life is good enough, right? You think our baby would be better off in some stranger's house? You've been hanging around Annie's for weeks. I'll have to tell her how much you really think of us."

Loretta put her hands over her face. He'd gotten her there—any mention of Annie would do it. He sometimes thought that she loved her more than him.

"Luther, we're seventeen," she said after a moment. "We don't know anything."

"We knew enough to do this. We did it and it must be right. You're not so helpless as you want to act like you are, Loretta. You're a spoiled little coward. I didn't know that about you."

Loretta ate many eggrolls after that evening, but she never split one open again, dislodging the curled shrimp inside, without remembering that inner shape that had once been inside her, without remembering that night.

After that meeting, she had only managed to see Annie once more before she left. For someone who had heard of everything, Annie could not understand the concept of where Loretta was being sent.

"You mean, you don't know anybody there? And they keep your baby?" she asked Loretta when she told her, and she solemnly shook her head, Yes, that's what she meant.

Annie did not offer to take the baby herself but said, "You've got to bear it, honey. Don't think you can get out of that."

Loretta had nodded, assuming she was talking about abortion, not yet legal in Ohio, but later she was not so sure. Perhaps Annie had meant that there was no separating yourself from a baby, even through legal means. But Loretta, who could not bear to consider this, changed the topic and asked her why she was rolling up her clothes before she put them into a suitcase for a trip to her sister's in Cleveland.

"If you roll them up, they don't get wrinkled," Annie said.

Loretta stood back and watched as she wrapped her black pumps in an old *Herald News* that had featured homecoming photos of Elaine Johnson that autumn. As Annie moved about the room, Loretta picked up one of the pumps and read around it, the description of Elaine's dress and the quote from her father, Junior Johnson. "We're proud but not surprised," he'd said.

Loretta had been at homecoming the night Elaine was chosen queen, her first and last public appearance with Luther. She'd met him in the bleachers, hoping her family, a dozen rows up in another section, wouldn't see who she was with. She sat beside Luther, too nervous to watch the action, and got up several times to go to the concession area bathroom.

She had always loved the concessions, the fathers in their bright sweaters hawking the pinkest of hot dogs. But she didn't see them that night, nor the girls her age huddled around the dim glass in the bathroom, corsages blooming from their breasts. Luther hadn't said a word about going with him to the after-game dance.

The last time she climbed back up to the stands, the crowd was standing as the queen was driven around the circular drive. The blacks in the audience were whooping at the sight of Elaine, and by the time Loretta reached Luther they were doing more than that—their fists were in the air and they were chanting, "Black power, black power!" Loretta turned around again to see if she could find her parents, but all she could see was the white disc of her brother's head. She wanted to put her fist up too, but her arm felt anchored at her side.

"This is great," she said instead, to Luther, who looked down at her from the great distance that was his height as if he'd never seen her in his life.

As they walked down the bleachers at the end of the game, they were followed too closely by a light-skinned black man with an elegant woman on his arm. Loretta felt he was nudging them along; when she turned around to look at him, she was surprised at his vivid scowl.

"Bad as his daddy," he hissed at Luther when they reached the bottom of the stairs.

"Who was that?" Loretta asked when they were alone again at his car.

Luther slammed into his side and left her standing in the dark.

"Who was he?" she asked again when he grudgingly unlocked her door.

"Elaine Johnson's father," he said and started the car with a roar.

CHAPTER 3

THEY'D NAMED HER Kay, but when she was older, she objected to being called simply by a letter.

"Would you want to be called M?" she asked her mother, who signed her full name Mrs. Marcia Milner, a trio of M's. Marcia said no; she usually said no. Her adopted daughter unnerved her. She never knew what was going to come out, or from where.

Marcia Milner had adopted Kay during her midlife crisis, which had commenced in her twenty-seventh year. She'd heard women saying they were still having theirs far into their fifties, but unless you knew the year of your death, who could say what was your middle. In any case, she was certain that hers had begun in 1970, when she and her husband, Marlon, in a fit of impetuousness and desperation and liberal good feeling had adopted a half-black child.

"But why don't they call them half-white?" she'd asked the social worker, one of many such questions she'd thrust across the room. "It's like saying a glass is half empty, as if black is negative and should be stressed first."

"That's your interpretation," the social worker said with a thin smile. She was already weary of Marcia Milner, with her bell-bottom pants and vivid red lips and social work degree of her own.

None of the four children she'd found for the Milners had passed Mrs. Milner's inspection, although she had been expansive in describing what she'd take beforehand, delivering long monologues on social responsibility. But, in fact, the social worker recognized Marcia Milner as simply one of many newly desperate women of her age and time, who after years of foam spermicide and uterine scrapings had found themselves leaning toward thirty and quite barren after all.

"Well, in any case, I'm sure you're going to love this one. She's the color of coffee au lait and has bright green eyes."

Marcia Milner jangled her charm bracelet in appreciation of the social worker's lyricism, although upon seeing the baby, she would have said cinnamon herself. All of the baby was this same matte tint, and to top it off, she had gripped instantly onto Marcia's thumb.

That was when Marcia'd decided—at the feel of that hot hand around her own stout thumb, which would never be duplicated further.

Even Marlon had no idea how hard it had been to forgo her own dreams of procreation. She had grown up with the strong idea that her traits, remixed, rethrown, might in the future produce someone spectacular. It wasn't going to be her; she realized this by her twenties. She saw that she wouldn't do much more than she had already managed—a college degree, a few strong papers, a series of campus demonstrations where she had stood in the forefront, glad for a reason to finally scream out about something. Being a redhead and a diabetic, she felt that she had wilted early, from too little insulin, from too much smoking and sun. She felt, even in her late teens, that time was running out.

Because of this, she didn't even consult Marlon when they first saw the baby, but said, "We'll take her," as if Kay had been a dress, and a bargain.

Because she had long suspected she was inferior, Marcia had specialized in counseling retarded adults. She felt superior there, at least, with these institutionalized, baby-faced women who chain-smoked Kools and guzzled Tab and let her tell them anything she wanted. For years, it was nearly as good as being a mother in earnest.

"Alma, you can't wear shorts and thongs for a job interview," she murmured automatically on her last day on the job. "And if you insist on wearing rouge, we're going to have to arrange a makeup consultation so you don't show up looking like a clown."

"What do you wear, Mrs. Milner?" Alma asked, standing beside the desk with her Buster Brown hairdo, all 195 pounds of her redolent with Tabu cologne.

"Blush-on. Max Factor. Look in my purse," Marcia said, frowning over a form.

Alma rifled through the bag while Marcia finished a

report for the social worker who would be taking over her caseload. Alma's vocational prospects were easy to reduce to a couple of categories: housekeeping or sheltered workshop assembly lines.

Now that she was a mother in earnest, Marcia planned to devote all of herself that there was to her daughter. She had values to instill, ideals to teach, while she could still remember what they were. Her future spread before her, lit by golden light, and in it she was always bent over, imparting.

In five minutes, Marlon would pick her up for the final time from this job—Marlon and Kay—everyone she cared about encased in their late model car. By tomorrow she'd be padding around Kay's pink bedroom in her slippers—she'd throw these damnable pumps out the door. A shiver of pleasure ran through her at the thought of this safe, maternal harbor. Bathed in these feelings, she allowed herself a benevolent glance at poor, outcast Alma, who had been rooting through her makeup bag and was now brandishing her blush.

"Not on your nose, Alma," she said, with a gentle smile. "Your nose is already prominent enough."

Six months later, Marcia Milner sat in her breakfast nook and leafed through the already well-worn *Dictionary of Childhood Illnesses*. She had not thought to buy this book until later, after she had already read the more esoteric volumes she had around the house. She had highlighted long sections in *Creative Childrearing* and a large, edited edition entitled *The Challenge of Motherhood*, but none of that seemed relevant now.

Kay had been endlessly sick since her adoption, with an array of illnesses that Marcia's mother noted primly Marcia'd never had. Croup, in a variety of manifestations, had dominated their first months together—Marcia's first truly free months since college. Those weeks, which she had imagined spent in sun-drenched rooms with a cooing infant, had instead been long gray hours filled with the low, alto baying of her hope, her daughter.

She'd already spent a large part of her savings taking Kay to the doctor, an old pediatrician who had offices down the block, offices she'd never even noticed before. But now many mornings she was sitting in the parking lot waiting for him to arrive.

"Dr. Moss!" she accosted him in the driveway with Kay bundled up like a secret.

"You really have to call before you show up, Mrs. Milner," the doctor said sourly. "At least wait until we're in the office."

Fevers, rashes, allergies to formula—obviously it wasn't Marcia's fault that she couldn't breastfeed the child—Dr. Moss filled up sheets with Kay's ailments, while Marcia rifled through *Childhood Illnesses* each night. But worst of all, Kay didn't seem comforted by her mother. When Marcia picked her up, her crying only increased as if she had been touched by fire.

Marcia stood over Kay's bed stonefaced each night when Marlon returned, chronicling her day of frustration.

"You saw how she grabbed hold of me that first day. Now she doesn't even like me to pick her up."

"What did you expect?" Marlon asked his wife. "She's a baby, for God's sake. This is how babies are."

"No," Marcia insisted. "It's because she isn't really mine."

Marcia hadn't even bothered photographing Kay's first smile, it had been so fleeting, and had possibly been a grimace anyway, associated with her constant gas. She hadn't chronicled her crawling, since it only preceded her knocking over something precious and shattering it.

She admitted aloud only to Dr. Moss that she might have made a serious mistake with this adoption, but even he didn't want to hear such confessions. He had grown so tired of Marcia Milner's strained face week after week that he had adjusted his office hours to after lunch in an effort to avoid her.

"I'm afraid that's all water under the bridge now, Mrs. Milner," he told her. "She's yours now and you're just going to have to do your best."

At home, Marcia studied the adoption papers, but they had reduced Kay's natural parents to objects of a certain size and color. She had dreams of discovering them on some sidewalk, of walking up to a 6'1" black silhouette, a 5'5" white one, and having them unite and absorb their child. She became convinced that the black man was a sociopath, the white girl a depressive, and that this was already the root of Kay's problems.

"How can I be responsible for years of aberrant behavior that I don't even understand?" she asked Marlon, who had grown so increasingly alarmed over his wife's wild theories and maternal ineptness that he finally encouraged her to go back to her job.

But Marcia discovered that her agency had gone through reorganization during her absence and that her position had been dissolved. She no longer had any space to glide into, like a boat. She had become fond of nautical terms—*unmoored* was a favorite.

In fact, one of the few people she still recognized at the office was Alma, neat and groomed in a floral housedress, who happened by to pick up a paycheck just as Marcia was leaving.

"Mrs. Milner, I bought Max Factor Blush-on too. Toasted Plum!"

Marcia found Alma so adjusted that it took her a moment to locate her position of superiority.

"Well, just use a lighter hand with it and you'll be fine," Marcia said finally. "Do you have a job?"

"Assistant housekeeper at Ramada Inn." As Alma opened her envelope and showed her the check, Marcia felt a sudden stab of bitter envy.

"I hope you're budgeting. Remember what I told you. Don't blow it all on treats and gum."

"I'm not," Alma said flatly, a bit belligerently, Marcia thought. "This is my last one anyhow. It was just for six months."

"Look at people when you talk to them, Alma. And don't flap that check in front of everyone unless you want to have it stolen."

Alma folded the check solemnly, then raised her eyes and asked, "Are you working here again, Mrs. Milner?"

Marcia snapped her bag shut, which was hanging open, displaying a muddle of cigarettes and disposable diapers.

"No," she said. "I just stopped by, actually—to see how things were going."

"I think they're going fine."

"Yes . . . well, keep in touch, Alma. I'm glad I saw you. And remember, don't slouch."

She was halfway down the hall when Alma called after her, "How's your baby? I forgot to tell you—I got me a certificate in child care now!"

CHAPTER 4

BEFORE SHE'D LEFT for the home for unwed mothers, Loretta had made her family a number of promises, not the least of which was that she'd never again be with anyone black. She had still been at the stage when she would have promised anything to get out of her trouble, but there had been no such chance. The tender region where she'd just discovered sex had become the site of numerous invasions: the silver thrust of speculums, the rubbery hands of foreign men. It had become a wound, and she would just as soon have had it sewn up for all the trouble it had caused her.

The two elderly women who ran the United Methodist Home for Unwed Mothers claimed to be virgins, although one hinted at a checkered past before Jesus entered her life. The way she said *entered* made it sound as if he had actually walked into her house. Jesus was the only man ever discussed in the home, a vaguely local kind of Jesus, whose girlish portraits hung in the hallways, his chestnut pageboy picked out by special lights.

The women worked themselves into a fervor contemplating him during the daily religious services; talk of his blood and loss brought low cries from their throats. Compared to him, the offending fathers of the pregnant girls were interlopers and oafs; the girls unspeakably weak, irretrievably tainted, compared to the women of the Bible, compared to these women themselves.

Many of the girls were quickly converted; it made life easier, month to month. They got the best beds and the largest portions and were more likely to be called to the phone when their boyfriends called. Luther hadn't even asked for the number; Loretta couldn't imagine him being interested in anyone in another area code.

By vacating the scene, Loretta saw that she had ended their relationship, at least for now. Their furtiveness was gone, for one thing, their exploits out in the light, where they could be picked up and judged by anyone. They were even open to a stranger like Miss Gibbons, headmistress of the home, who had scanned Loretta's entry application the first week she was there with obvious relish.

"So your relationship with this Biggs person, was it a long-term situation?"

"Long enough," Loretta said, shifting in the prisoner's chair. "It would have been longer, but I had to leave."

Miss Gibbons leveled her with a meaningful glance. Under her papery lids, Loretta thought she caught the eye of a fanatic.

"And your parents knew about it, of course."

Loretta crossed her legs with difficulty. "No."

"They didn't know of it at all, or they didn't know he was black?"

Loretta had filled out this form herself and knew there were no such questions.

"You'll have to ask them exactly what they knew," she said. "Their phone number's right there."

She would have liked to have said more. In fact, what she would have liked to have said was lodged in an ever-growing clot in her throat—departing remarks to girls in her home ec class who smirked over their recipes her last day of class, although they'd had plenty of sex themselves with blond boys who had pimples on their necks; she would have liked to have left a departing volley to her typing teacher, the spidery Miss Cutler, who'd begun hanging over her during typing tests once word of Luther leaked out.

"Faster! Faster!" she prompted, as Loretta typed, over and over, "The fat cat ate the bad rat. The fat cat . . ."

What she wanted to say to her parents, however, could not be found. It seemed settled in some interior sediment and only boiled up when she cried.

But she only cried once before she left, in her parents' bedroom, making her mother take her into her arms—an explosion of snot and tears and incoherence—and that was the closest she came to communicating anything to anyone.

Yet even though Loretta kept her mouth shut, Miss Gibbons clearly marked her as a troublemaker, using her as an example of willfulness of the wicked variety.

Loretta was the only girl who wouldn't stand for the Benediction on a particular Sunday; this was because of a wave of belated morning sickness rather than belligerence, but Loretta didn't correct her.

You couldn't correct her anyhow; Miss Gibbons's views, arcane and bizarre, seemed frozen in her appropriately narrow face. Loretta thought of a collie when she looked at her, of how she had read once that, because of overbreeding, collies' heads had grown so slender that their brains were the size of a pea.

She had many such renegade, unchristian thoughts, more than usual with so much time on her hands. *Time on her hands.* She understood that saying for the first time, along with others, direct from her grandmother and aunts—grin and bear it, for example.

Sitting outside Miss Gibbons's paneled office, she heard her use the word *attitude* repeatedly while giving Loretta's parents her three-month progress report. She was certainly making progress—she was big as a horse—but Miss Gibbons was speaking of the spiritual variety.

She didn't know that Loretta's parents were leery of such strident devoutness and wouldn't much care what she said on this topic.

"But is she eating?" Loretta heard her mother ask, and Miss Gibbons gave a harsh laugh. "You don't have to worry about that."

Given the bland and tiny servings at the home, eating was uppermost in Loretta's mind, and her parents' visits were the occasion for great gorging out in the world. Nothing but a bout of Methodist forbearance could make a foot-long hotdog taste so good.

Only after Loretta ate her fill at whatever restaurant her parents took her to did she allow herself to notice the sidelong glances they received. Accompanying their lumbering, outcast daughter, her parents walked stiffly, but with their heads held high. Taking her cue from them, Loretta raised her own chin and made herself vow never to forget this, their surprising grace under pressure.

As the weeks went by, Loretta tried to see her pregnancy as a strictly physical condition, some viral trouble that took nine months to pass. Miss Gibbons encouraged this, treating the body as a treacherous arena that should be either curbed or ignored. There was no informational material in the home about pregnancy, only *The Upper Room* and *The Christian Teen*, both carted in by local women who volunteered for devotional counseling. Loretta recognized the type from her hometown church, Unity Methodist, stiff do-good women who were bored at home.

"I don't have anything to be saved from," she told the blond housewife who, with whispered instructions, had been specially assigned to her. She had taken up knitting as a steadying activity for tense moments like these. She clacked her needles energetically; there were moments when she feared she might explode.

The woman viewed her with an appropriately

pitying expression, full of the background material Miss
Gibbons had provided.

"Jesus forgives *all* sins," she said meaningfully, and
Loretta switched to purl—she was knitting nothing, an
aimless trail of green—and muttered, "Leave me alone."

She was on her own in a way she had never been
before. There was no use forming friendships with the
other girls—they arrived and departed on such a regular
basis—but a kind of boot camp camaraderie developed,
rife with gossip. Someone started the rumor that if you
had sex after your first conception, it was possible to
be doubly pregnant, and that your second fetus wouldn't
start growing until the first one was born.

This thought—that the process she was undergoing
might be immediately duplicated—was so sobering that
it haunted Loretta, until she realized that Miss Gibbons
had probably been the person who started it, with just
that intent.

"I'd do anything to get out of here," Loretta wrote
on a pad one summer night, then had no one to send it
to, except Louis, and she was scared he would show
their parents. Long before her departure, her mother
had proclaimed that he had fallen under Loretta's influ-
ence, as if under the wheels of a speeding car.

As proof she had marched into his room and returned
with a *Jet* magazine that had James Brown and the Famous Flames on the cover. Loretta had laughed out loud
at the sight—one of the Flames was throwing a magenta
cape over the singer's back.

"I never told him to buy that," she said.

"You don't have to tell him anything. He picks it all up."

"Well, excuse me," Loretta had snapped. "Maybe I should go off somewhere and die."

This, of course, was before she was pregnant, when such scenes were still possible. Pregnancy had pulled the plug on such encounters, had revealed her false power. For all her ranting and insolence, she was a seventeen-year-old white girl with a talent for French kissing and a vinyl purse full of dimes.

In the last week of July, Loretta picked up a sewing machine on the basis of dorm room gossip that if you lifted something heavy it would bring on your child. It was ready to come now; she could feel it. Little fists seemed to beat on her walls; there were belligerent kicks in the night. Loretta imagined her baby's impatience as equal to hers. These were the dog days of summer; they were both anxious to get on with their lives.

She woke one morning in August to a soft weight like a melon between her legs and went to Miss Gibbons, who pursed her lips and asked—hopefully, Loretta thought—"Do you have any pain?"

But Loretta felt no pain, only a pressure, and this made her confident that, in her personal case, labor would be a breeze.

Miss Gibbons drove her off to the hospital in her ancient Chevy, a jaunty scarf about her neck, while Loretta looked around innocently at the bright morning, thinking that by the next day this would be done.

After they parked, Miss Gibbons gave her a Gideon as a departing present and said, "We'll phone your parents in the lobby," as she took her arm.

It was then that Loretta felt her first foreboding of pain; a wide arc of it swept across her stomach. When it passed, she steadied herself, as if she were the old woman, and let Miss Gibbons lead her on.

"I don't want to call them until it's over," she managed; she saw that it was entirely possible that she'd be creating quite a racket later on.

Loretta hadn't screamed out loud since she was a little girl and boys had chased her through her yard. She hadn't even known she could still do it, but she soon found that she could, and well. Strapped to a narrow cot in a white room, she could barely believe her own howls. But they were hers all right, and so frequent that the nurse became annoyed.

"You're not the only one, you know," she said smartly, and Loretta bit her arm without aplomb.

Miss Gibbons had called her parents, so they were privy to these outcries. Loretta realized this dimly around the eighteenth hour of labor, when her father evidently tried to come in to her and was stopped by the doctor.

"Hold on there, Daddy. She's almost done."

Loretta heard her father obey; rather, she did not hear him protest—they were an obedient family, at the bottom. Loretta found the knowledge of her parents' presence more excruciating than the physical pain. Miss Gibbons had gotten her, after all.

When she woke, her stomach was gone and she was trussed up like a turkey. The relief on her mother's face when she walked into the recovery room was so vast, it was as if someone had taken an eraser and wiped away the pain. But underneath, Loretta saw that she'd changed her—she had caused her own mother grief. Even more than being pregnant, she saw this as her first dire act.

She was placed in the maternity ward with three other mothers whose babies nursed noisily as calves. The contents of her body were not mentioned again until the next day when a social worker brought a ream of adoption papers that she was advised not to read too closely. Loretta had rarely signed anything official before this; she was still too young for a credit card or a loan. She leafed through the legal words until she found the dotted line; there was no space here for Luther.

When she returned home the next week, Loretta found that her mother had stockpiled a new yellow wardrobe in her absence: skirts and sweaters and slacks, all mix and match.

Loretta wore a yellow blouse, skirt and sandals the last time she saw Luther, when he picked her up at the corner of her house a few days after her return.

It should have been a solemn moment, but he laughed when she walked up to the car.

"You look like a canary," he said as she opened the door.

He wanted to look her in the face, and finally reached

out for her chin and pivoted it his way. Loretta kept her eyes averted—she felt more virginal than before she'd left.

"I'm married now," Luther said finally.

"To who?"

"Elaine Johnson," he said, moving away.

Loretta had been called expectant for so long that it was hard for her to register that this time was now over. She saw that she had wanted something further from Luther: in her yellow outfit, bought by her mother, she had meant to captivate him all over again. But she was heading away from this place now, and captivation, even if it were possible, would have done her no good.

"Did you get to see her?" Luther asked, referring to the baby, who they both assumed was a girl.

Loretta shook her head.

"You didn't even ask?"

"They say it's harder if you do."

"Harder." He laughed, a dark note, then said, "I'm having another one, with Elaine."

Loretta opened the car door; it seemed the thing to do. "Well, you'll get to see that one, at least," she said.

When Loretta thought about it (she didn't like to think about it), she had first gone to a plastic surgeon not long after this encounter, during her first quarter in college. Something dire had happened to her face in the last year, but no one else seemed to notice.

"What exactly do you think's wrong with you?" the doctor asked, once she was in his office.

118

Loretta tilted up her face and murmured, "Around my eyes."

There were circles there, for one thing, which she covered with camouflage cream, and underneath, if you looked closely, a delicate network of lines.

"Infants have lines under their eyes—you've had those since you were born," the doctor said. "Something else must be wrong with you."

Loretta balked at this suggestion; she considered such comments outside his realm. She was charged fifty dollars for this odd interlude, but had them bill her at a wrong address under an erroneous name.

She did this again, at intervals, with different doctors, throughout her years at college. Her face vexed her; it was the one map that illustrated clearly where she had been.

She had gotten this notion from Annie, from whom so many of her notions sprung. A prostitute named Miss Moses lived next door to her on Sugar Street and occasionally came over to use the phone when Loretta was there.

Miss Moses wore red dresses over long, dry legs and had a face that hung under rouge like a steak.

"That's what too much life will do to you," Annie commented. "That's what you look like when men treat you bad."

But Loretta did not let men treat her badly. She picked and took them, picked and took them, like fruit from a tree. In between this, she read. She was in college, after all, receiving what was called, to her pleasure, a liberal arts degree. This meant that for twelve weeks her brain absorbed parliamentary government, agnosticism, the sexual life of bees. After each semester, these facts vacated her, as if she had been picked up and shaken by the feet.

But she couldn't take seriously all the avid young students (white boys, Luther would have called them) with their ponytails and carefully battered jeans. Loretta sampled them—this was the word she chose (she took literature, too, for two semesters in a row once, due to a scheduling irregularity). She had an IUD shoved into her uterus while the gynecologist explained that nobody knew why they worked, but they had been used successfully with camels.

She had finally been propelled clear of Union, her one great dream, and now was lost, anonymous, just another girl on the street. She didn't call Luther or Annie, though their number felt engraved on her face. The facts of their address—21 Sugar Street—would sometimes rise up in the middle of a pop quiz or when she was in the arms of one of the endless young men.

One in particular, named Dan, was fascinated with her, chiefly because he couldn't figure out her aloofness.

"Don't you want to get married and have kids? I never met a girl who didn't want to settle down."

But Loretta had scrambled the natural order of things, evidently. "I already had my child, and she's gone from me. What's the point of settling down now?"

She didn't mention the color of her child until later,

when Dan unsuspectingly called a basketball player he was watching on television a spade.

Loretta turned off the TV and gave him his jacket. "My daughter's half-black," she told him. "When you call someone that, it's the same to me as if you were talking to her."

Loretta was strangely unattached to these relationships; she was generally unattached. Whenever she became fond of something, it was an inanimate object. She cried profusely when she had to give up her Pontiac Tempest, a blue dented model that her father had bought her for two hundred dollars without noticing that underneath the ratty front carpet there was virtually no floor.

"We'll get you another car, Loretta," he said when she wept to him on the phone.

"But not like that one; there's only one like that one," and even as she was saying this, Loretta knew she was grieving for something else.

CHAPTER 5

ANNIE BIGGS HAD her own signs and portents: hearing a mourning dove first thing in the morning was good luck, hearing an owl last thing at night was bad. She knew birds and the messages they conveyed and cultivated them, especially the little ones with red and pink at their breasts. She bought special seed for the finches and tits and robins—she liked their little movements, their lack of spectacle. Her kids had never gotten over seeing swans fly, the hurricane whoosh of their great span, but Annie wasn't interested in such noise and flap.

She let animals overrun her house—*overrun* was the word of her neighbors. Raccoons ate her garbage. "Who else is gonna eat it?" she asked. She allowed spiders to live in her bathroom window so that she could watch the slow crocheting of their webs. On days when she didn't feel like moving, when she wanted to pull the blinds at nine and simulate another night, she would be pulled out of it eventually not by human intervention, but by the pecking of a pileated woodpecker on the half-dead crabapple she wouldn't allow to be cut, by the busy feet of squirrels rolling acorns across her rotted roof.

Luther liked to say that when he had money, he would redo the house from top to bottom, but she would never allow it. Too many creatures depended on it, let alone him.

"Mama, we have bats," he had told her just this morning, after a night when she had heard him and Elaine murmuring all night. It was obvious that Elaine was pregnant again, although her daughter-in-law had not yet told her. She kept her lips pursed, as if with a bright red snap.

"Where?"

"In the attic. Elaine wanted me to get some of Roman's old baby clothes and one just about flew in my mouth."

"You gotta learn to keep your mouth shut," Annie said with a smile, wondering, as she always wondered, what would make this boy of hers happy. Obviously not another child.

"We can't have bats flying around here," he said, suddenly annoyed. "They get in your hair."

"They're not thinking about your hair. They're hanging upside down, minding their own business."

There was silence for two beats, then three.

"What'd Elaine want baby clothes for?"

But he still didn't want to tell her. What did he think, that he and his sister had been planned on some calendar, that she and his father, Horace, had said a word of what they were expecting when they crawled on all fours into bed each night. She had let Horace think what he wanted, and she did the same when they burrowed under the covers. Neither knew up until the end of their brief marriage what the other had hoped.

Luther turned away, but he didn't leave the room. He stood in the entrance, fiddling with the doorknob, as if he were thinking of taking it off.

"How far along is she?"

He took his hand off the round black orb. "I don't know. Four, five months, I guess."

"There'll be time for you to play basketball on the weekends, baby," she told him. "You better decide how you're gonna support all this mess."

Luther was cutting Netty's hair in her bathroom the next week when he said, "I should do this for a job."

"Do what, cut hair?"

"Yeah. Why not?"

Netty looked up at her brother in the mirror; she didn't feel like looking at herself. Although she blamed it on the fluorescent lighting in her bathroom, her face of late appeared to sag.

"I'm not saying anything. I'm just surprised."

Luther had only cut half of her bangs, but he laid down the scissors.

"Nobody's ever known how to do black hair in this town. Damn, why didn't I think of it before?"

"Don't you have to go to school to get a license?"

"So, I'll go to school if I have to. I'm good at it! I've been cutting hair since I was a boy."

"Okay, okay," Netty said. "Finish mine now, will you?"

She was a bit jaded about Luther's schemes; he'd had so many of them. Not that she was being critical; she knew the importance of dreams. She kept up a few of her own, watching hopefully throughout the years whenever a new man she met picked up her son, Andre, hoping to see something in his eyes. But there had been nothing so far, and Andre was turning ten, too big for anyone to pick up. So big, in fact, that the men she knew showed only plain disappointment at the sight of the miniature man Andre had become standing at the front door when she came home at night.

On those evenings, Netty took great pains to masquerade as someone she was no longer certain she was —a single woman, leaning toward thirty, who still had a certain verve and zest. She made sure to take a nap after supper so that she could dance until late, to leave an extra few minutes for false eyelashes; otherwise her eyes seemed to recede into her head. And she bought several long-line girdles like her mother's that encased her trunk and culminated in a binding brassiere that pushed up her breasts. Otherwise, she couldn't fit into the tight acetate dresses she had bought years ago for such occasions and that she could not afford to update or replace.

But being so restrained, she couldn't eat on these evenings, unless she wanted cramps. Sometimes she got them anyway, lying next to a man she had already given up on by midnight. Not one of them ever stayed up after sex to rub her feet or listen to her talk about her assembly line job; instead, they kept her awake with their snores. She didn't allow this often, partly for Andre's sake, partly her own. A full night's lost sleep affected her for days afterward. She seemed unable to make it up. She still had dreams about a math final she had missed in high school, when she was first pregnant with Andre. The teacher, a papery white woman named Miss Dodd, had turned away from her when she'd come to take it later on.

"That test is over, Miss Biggs," she said smartly. "You're going to have to learn that there are things you just can't make up."

Netty had learned this, along with much else, and so allowed herself only the occasional indulgence. But she wouldn't discourage her brother, whatever he wanted.

As he finished her hair, she made herself smile up at him in the mirror. "Go on and do it," she told him.

But Luther changed his mind after seeing the dim corridors of Midwestern Beauty Academy. Netty accompanied him to registration and suspected it was all the white girls who'd cinched it, droves of them, all looking like Brenda Lee with their towering hair and sooty eyes. Luther was so busy avoiding their burning cigarettes in the crowded hallways that he didn't notice that these girls were, in fact, dodging the two of them.

No one else black, and no other man, graced these gray halls, but Netty didn't care.

As soon as they sat down in the back of a room for the orientation by a large, caped woman named Nonny Rae Mason, Netty felt the surge of pleasure and hopefulness she always found in a school setting.

As soon as Mrs. Mason launched into her lecture—the Coiffure Across the Ages—Luther rose with a disgusted hiss, but Netty stayed on. She joined him back at the car forty-five minutes later, where he was staring up at a line of moldering brick buildings, already set on another plan.

"There's some fund for renovating old buildings like this—I read about it in the paper. You know how good I've always been with my hands—"

Netty listened with half an ear as they drove back home. Apart from practicalities, such as money, it sounded more plausible. She couldn't imagine Luther standing stationary, day after day, his hands in hair. But she could imagine it for herself and had done so so suddenly that her change of direction made her breathless.

"I'm going to do it, then," she said.

"Do what?"

"Enroll. Learn how to do hair."

They had an old family look that they used to pass each other as children, when one or the other was surprising or sly. Luther didn't give it to her for a moment, but then there it was, out of the corner of his eye.

"Well, go on then, girl! And the first building I do

will be for you!" And they both laughed out loud into the autumn air, miraculously enlivened.

Although Luther had no particular training for his new venture, he hit a vein of luck that made up for it instead. He teamed up with a Muslim entrepreneur in the neighborhood, and together they bid on two rows of crumbling structures on the edge of downtown. All that needed to be approved now was a small business loan, and it showed signs of being passed with surprising swiftness. Overnight, Luther saw the light at the end of his tunnel. He'd faced so many obstacles, but whoever was testing him had evidently decided it was time for them to end. He had business cards made up that read BIGGS BUILDERS, just for the look of it, then penned in RENOVATORS on the bottom to make them entirely true.

He applied first to renovate the building that had housed Wong's Chinese Palace, which closed after seven years of the grand opening special: wonton soup, eggroll, and chicken chow mein for $3.99. It had become clear during this time that the Wong daughter wasn't going to flourish in the Union school system. Someone started the rumor that she was Mongolian, which people thought meant retarded. She was so ostracized that the family finally moved to friendlier waters.

Luther asked Annie to cosign the loan for him, which meant she would lose her house if he didn't keep up the payments. Luther assured her he would never do this, one of the first times he'd assured her of anything.

"I love this house, Mama. I'd never do that to you. Plus, I'm gonna make it now. Big."

It was clear that Elaine didn't share his optimism about the business. She'd become pregnant again before regaining her old shape, roaming the house in the same maternity clothes she seemed to have been wearing now for years. Being confined at Annie's had taken its toll; she'd grown not only melancholy but prone to confrontation.

"You've never liked me, have you?" she asked Annie one afternoon when she was almost a week overdue.

Annie was making gravy over the stove and didn't turn away.

"Of course I like you, honey. What're you talking about?"

"But you liked that white girl, that Loretta, better. You wanted Luther to marry her."

"I wanted Luther to be happy. I never told him how to do it."

"Well, he's not now, that's for sure," Elaine said, sitting down gingerly, as if on a tack.

"He's getting himself squared away," Annie said in a low voice. "You all will do better once he's got a job."

"It won't be good, because we didn't start out right," Elaine muttered. "I even saw it that first day."

She broke off as Luther walked into the room in his bathrobe, although it was nearly noon and the middle of the week.

"What's the matter?" he asked his wife, feeling the friction in the air, and at his voice Annie let go of her spoon.

130

"I'll tell you what's wrong. She's having another baby too fast and she's got a husband moping around his mama's all day."

"Hey, wait a minute!" Luther said, backing up, clearly not expecting this.

"This is your life, Luther. You made it and you dragged this girl along. Now go get dressed and take her to the hospital. I'm too old to deliver a baby on my floor."

Luther's face changed as he looked closely at Elaine. She had placed both hands on her abdomen, as if it were a drum.

"You're ready?" he asked in disbelief; he'd lost all track of this somehow.

Elaine stood up in answer, as if called upon to recite.

"Come with us, Mama," he managed. He dreaded hospitals; Annie had passed this on to him, one of the few fears she'd named.

"I'm busy here with this gravy. You can handle it on your own."

Elaine walked out of the room, heading for her bedroom, but Luther stood still.

"Luther."

He turned.

"Put your arms around her before you go. It's hard work having a baby. This is the third one you caused, and it's time you realized that."

A week later, Annie went outside after Luther left to pick up his loan papers and sat on a lawn chair that had appeared several years ago, she did not know how.

Life went on at night on Sugar Street, and objects appeared and disappeared in the process under cover of dark. From her window, she heard transactions take place that she never witnessed in the light. She had once seen a woman slapped so hard in her adjoining alley that her head had swiveled, like an owl. Annie had shone a flashlight down on the perpetrator, but she couldn't recognize him or the woman, who fled down the gravel in her summer dress.

Scenes like this reminded Annie of why she had never struck up another serious relationship after Horace left her; she had become unable to muster the correct combination of hope and blindness that such liaisons required. When men over the years suggested they'd help her, that a woman shouldn't be in such a big house on her own, Annie would tell them that she wasn't alone, that she had her children, that she had her birds, that she had, at bottom, herself. No one actually believed that she could mean this, least of all Luther, who still showed up with an odd assortment of men at her door—pool-playing cronies and friends' fathers—anxious for them to sample Annie's meals and thereby be smitten by her. And although she fed these men—she'd feed anyone—she did so with a secret smile for the naiveté of her son, despite his swagger and suede.

That morning on the lawn with garbage cans chained around her, Annie sat with the sun aligned with her left ear, the moon at her right. Her finches rustled in the briars at the corner of her property, and her house sat behind her, Elaine and her newborns inside. They had turned out to be not only Luther's third but his fourth as well. Annie had named the twin girls Rose and Lily; Luther and Elaine had been too stunned. Annie sat there until the moon disappeared and the sun shifted and her own son returned from wherever he'd gone for the loan. Annie cosigned the papers from her chair with a red ballpoint pen.

"I guess you'll be leaving me now," she told him. "If you've got a business, you'll be able to get a place of your own."

Luther rolled up the papers and looked at the sky.

"I guess I will be," he said.

CHAPTER 6

"And to make it worse, I still haven't lost ten of the pounds I gained with Jonathan!" the woman told Marcia Milner in dramatic tones.

"Really?" Marcia asked absently, labeling this woman, this neighbor in her living room, as 503.3, weight disorder, obsessive type, then dipping back into her own reservoir of grisly thoughts, which she hoped would never be known, or labeled, by anyone.

She was trying to figure out how she could kill herself and then arrange for her body to be picked up before anyone in her family found her. She had her suicide well planned—a simple overdose of insulin—but her body, even dead, remained an issue.

"You didn't have that problem, did you? Your figure has always been so firm—"

"Kay's adopted," Marcia said flatly.

"Oh, that's right. Of course. I'm sorry."

Now that she was dislodged from her thoughts, Marcia Milner studied Marlene Vilgilanti with displeasure, dressed as she was in a mauve jogging suit and matching sneakers, although she clearly had no intention of running. These coffee hours with neighborhood mothers had been pressed on her by Marlon, who seemed at the end of whatever length of rope he'd been provided.

Marcia had nearly all she had hoped for—freedom, a child, and now Alma to help her. These things Marlon was funding. Marcia would have to take care of her peace of mind for herself.

"How's she doing, really?" Marlene asked, soto voce, meaning Alma, who was banging metal in the kitchen, since she insisted on cooking and cleaning along with taking care of Kay.

"She's fine," Marcia answered, although, in fact, Alma was superior. She daydreamed of leaving Marlon with her and her rolling pins forever, thinking he would probably be more satisfied.

Kay walked into the room then, all four feet of her, and announced. "I want some Kool-Aid, Marcia. Red."

"Tell Alma. Honey," Marcia added for the sake of company.

"I did. She says it's all gone."

"Well, then, she'll have to buy some when she goes shopping. Tell her to add it to the list."

"But I want some now. Why can't you go?" Kay insisted.

"Kay Rita!" Marcia raised her eyebrows in warning, but Kay merely plopped down in the middle of the floor, near Marlene Vilgilanti's well-shod foot, and dissolved into tears.

She did this everywhere, over everything—in a shopping mall because it was too big, in a restaurant because Marcia wouldn't allow her to put salt in her water, and in church, on the rare occasion Marcia made them all go, because she didn't like the pews. Marcia had never seen so much unhappiness, so readily displayed, as in Kay, who had browned alarmingly over the years, as if she were a muffin baked on low.

"Well." Marlene Vilgilanti extricated her shoe, which Kay had rolled onto in her tantrum. "I guess I should go and start supper. If you ever want to go to Weight Watchers—"

"I'll let you know," Marcia said, rising to walk her to the door. When she came back into the living room, she said, "Kay Rita Milner!" in the same voice her mother had once used with her. But what did Kay know of this tradition, this old voice of her white family, with freckles and diabetes and ingrown toenails in their background. She only wailed louder, until Alma dutifully appeared and picked her up.

"Oh, we're a little cranky one today, aren't we?" she said in cooing tones, not daring to look at Mrs. Milner, who had grown even more elevated in the last years, now not only a former counselor, but a boss.

"Oh, Christ," Marcia Milner said. "She's a pain in the ass, that's all." And Kay wrenched around to scream back, "Ass! Ass! Ass!" as she hung from Alma's arms.

Back when she was trapped in an office, Marcia had imagined a domestic life of contented activity, where she darned socks and cut crusts and washed down ceilings in her spare time. But, in fact, the more time she had on her hands, the less she seemed able to manage.

"Wieners, three nights in a row?" Marlon cried. "Marcia, what is your problem? You lie around all day, and then all you can pull together is minced horse hoofs and pig snouts? Is this how much you think of your family?"

Marcia had to restrain herself from telling him the truth—that, yes, it was how much she thought of them or anyone.

As a girl her idea of adulthood had actually centered on the procurement of food. This was freedom, meandering through a grocery with a cart and a billfold, swayed only by your own desires. She vowed to buy all the items her mother blithely passed by—golden cheese spread, invitingly artificial; pigs' feet pickled in brine; prebaked peach pies—an avalanche of junk. But the allure of this ended almost instantly after she had to start doing it. She wasn't feeding herself, after all—there were the others and the food groups and the budget to consider, let alone her slender culinary skills. Going to the grocery had now grown from a chore to a journey to a major event.

Even suicide seemed a more complex act than she could handle, and she couldn't keep from imagining the ramifications. For example, she didn't like to think about Marlon's fine prospects for finding another wife. She imagined him and a faceless other woman discussing her in the past tense; she didn't like to be talked about in any event, and the thought of these future conversations was more than she could stand.

And she was even more disinclined to fall out of grace with Alma, the one person she'd been able to mystify. Marcia had managed all the things in life that Alma had elevated to great prizes: a house of her own in which she could do whatever she pleased without permission from a supervisor; a husband who wore gold on his hand to signal his bondage and returned home each night as obedient as a dog; a refrigerator from which she could entirely consume anything she wanted. Alma, in her group home, would have none of these things, ever, and on the rare occasion when Marcia appreciated her life, it was because of Alma's point of view, right smack beside hers.

Kay, on the other hand, would only be baffled by her death, as she was baffled by her in life. Despite legal papers in the drawer, the girl never seemed entirely convinced that Marcia was her relative.

When she asked, "Why?" and Marcia said, "Because I say so and I'm your mother," it sounded feeble and weightless, like the lie it was.

By the time Kay was five, Marcia had given up entirely on almost every notion she had dragged into the process of adoptive motherhood. She was providing this little stranger with room and board and the not insubstantial assistance of Alma, who, being cast from certain realms of the world, was especially adept at others. And Marcia had the dubious pleasure of hearing Alma give Kay instructions that Marcia had once offered herself: "Don't chew gum, honey. It makes you look cheap. Stand up! Look at people when you talk to them."

When Marlon let Kay get a dog for her birthday, Marcia appropriated it for herself. She found that she was suited to a domestic animal; the commands were easy, the rewards fast. Some nights when Alma read to Kay, and Marlon stayed late at the office, as he progressively did, to Marcia's dim suspicion and alarm, Marcia watched TV in momentary contentment, a circle of yellow fur in her arms.

In her idleness, she asked for Alma's records, curious after all these years about exactly what was wrong. But under the labels and diagnoses, she found only one central fact—that Alma had been abandoned as an infant, given some obscure testing, then shunted from one institution to the other for the next twenty years of her life. She was called EMR now—Educably Mentally Retarded—but Marcia knew that half the world could be called that.

After reading the files, Marcia made an effort to take Alma out into the world, chiefly on outings to restaurants. This was an enormous thrill for Alma, who couldn't read the menu and would have had to choose by the photos had Marcia not been along. It gave Marcia a perverse pleasure to edit Alma's possibilities, to assure her, for example, that the only side dishes available were three-bean salad and beets. She justified herself by noting Alma's heft and certain cholesterol problems; why even allow her to know the existence of sausage gravy and hash browns? Marcia was practically her guardian, after all.

But although Alma was radiant for days over the

prospect of these trips, the actual experience rattled her. She would become riveted by the bubbling juice dispenser and the revolving dessert display, which she said made her want to cry.

"All that icing!" she exclaimed to Marcia, her eyes seeping under the Maybelline mascara she used for such outings.

Her coffee cup could only be filled to a certain level or she became upset and called back the waitress endlessly to adjust it. "Excuse me, please, excuse me!" she proclaimed every time a waitress, a waiter, or even a manager happened by. She did not understand that these workers were not paid to be her confidants.

"You don't tell complete strangers your life story," Marcia hissed after Alma snagged a placid-faced waitress one noon and spilled out that the reason she liked to collect half-and-half containers was that she'd only been given powdered milk in the state hospital.

"But why not? She looked interested," Alma asked, sulking over a double Big Boy drenched in a golden pond of processed cheese.

Marcia averted her eyes to her own prim plate—a chicken salad platter. She ate wisely in spite of herself, even though she wished to die.

"You just don't," she said smartly, an answer she also dished out to Kay, with even less success.

Alma looked at her painfully; it was obvious she just didn't get it. Marcia could teach her about emery boards and tampons, but some notions were just too complex.

These scoldings were a waste of time, in any event.

Alma forgot from one trip to another what it meant to be circumspect. Marcia stopped taking her to restaurants entirely after Alma went off to the Big Boy kitchen one afternoon and offered to personally help with the dishes; they had used so many of them, she felt.

Still, something in Marcia had given way and she no longer protested the odd bond between Alma and Kay. When she came in with her flat proud face and announced, "Kay can do her addition through ten!" Marcia now said, "Good," and half meant it.

CHAPTER 7

SINCE ELAINE JOHNSON had a house of her own, she liked to think "mine" whenever she walked through the door. She had given off doing that with her husband when he sank down on her at night or with her son, Roman, who had moved out of her arms into the dominion of boys. He now liked rocks and sticks and dirt and brought them in to her, on his clothes, in his hands. But her girls were still small enough to cuddle and she put an arm around each of them the first time she crossed the threshold of 541 W. Water.

Now that she had this place, her personality returned to her, like a phantom. She finally unpacked crates of high school clothes and tried them on for the pain they caused when they wouldn't zip. She opened up cartons of old school papers and studied Polaroids stuck in the pages of philosophy books. She missed her family.

She had received no communication from Junior and only holiday cards from her mother, signed with a distant affection: "Dear Elaine, I hope your family does something nice for your birthday." Helene didn't even know the extent of her so-called family, since Elaine had not sent a photograph of her children and she and Luther had rarely been captured on film.

By the time Elaine finally had the impulse to call her mother, the number Helene had given her years ago was answered by a man who sounded not only white but infirm.

"No Helene lives here," he told her.

"But she must. Is this Dock Street in Port Jefferson?"

"It's Port Jefferson, but it's not Dock. Who did you say you were?"

"Elaine," Elaine said stupidly. "My mother gave me this number."

"Well, I've had it three years at least. I can't talk anymore."

After the man hung up, Elaine moved to the mirror in the hall. It was April seventeenth, 2:08 in the afternoon, and she couldn't imagine where she'd been all this time. What she knew now showed plainly; no clever makeup could mask it. She recognized her look in other women she'd never seriously studied before, in women like Netty, who'd once seemed so jaded and old. She even saw it in Annie as she watched Luther walk out the door.

When she was a girl, Elaine had watched Roy Rogers's mother on "This Is Your Life"—a woman so tiny and shriveled and worn out from having Roy Rogers and all his sisters that she couldn't stand up. The father was still hale and hearty, clapping Ralph Edwards on the back. Even then Elaine remembered thinking, "I'll never get used up like that."

And here she had. Sometimes when her children pulled down on her coat sleeves, Elaine felt like giving in to their downward tug and curling up on her linoleum floor.

Women who bore children before they were themselves yet knew something she'd never heard put into words. She wished she'd paid more attention to this before she'd had three by the time she was twenty-five years old.

Luther was obviously annoyed with her when he came into the house after work, without the greeting scent of supper in the air.

"But you've had that number for years, and you've never tried to call her," he said when she explained what was wrong.

Elaine shook her head as if it was too painful to form a reply; she was sitting over a scattering of blue stationery at the dining room table—each sheet with a word or two written on the top line. Luther leaned over and read, "Helene, Dear Mother, Mom."

She knew that this was the way she had treated him years ago, when he'd first tried to approach her. She had shaken her head at his tender words, as if he were speaking a foreign language.

"Maybe it'll be forwarded if you write," he tried, while behind them Rose reached up to the counter for a box of cookies, obviously hungry.

"If not, I'll just have to get ahold of Daddy," Elaine said as she began writing again.

"Shit," Luther said, missing the box, which fell to the floor and spilled out into a line of cracked chocolate.

Luther now had almost everything he needed: a wife, three children, a house, a business, a car, and a variety of loans. It was typical that with all this assembled, the primary element would start to falter. He had been so busy concentrating on his own destiny that he hadn't paid much attention to Elaine, who had begun to act as if she didn't want his attentions anyway.

Her lack of response would have alarmed him if he hadn't been so tired. He hadn't felt like this since years ago, with Loretta. In fact, Annie had taken his great fatigue as the first sign that Loretta was pregnant.

"You gave one of your good seeds," she explained to him. "You're gonna feel as tired as she does."

But he had presumably spent equally good seed with Elaine, and Annie never explained why he hadn't felt that way again. Her theories had no obvious basis; you either believed them or not, and he usually did.

Even Elaine's one request, that they have a home of their own, had been granted without visible excitement on her part. He had wanted her to help make the few choices that they could afford. Did she prefer brick or wood, a ranch or a duplex? But Elaine didn't seem to know. She had accompanied him to look at houses as if she were one of his children, hanging back from the real estate agent with his bright plaids and loud words.

"Does your wife want an eat-in kitchen or a dining room?" the man asked Luther in one home, and he had to backtrack to find Elaine, standing at the living room window, to ask in a whisper.

It was embarrassing not to have her now at the point when he needed her. He even had to talk her into coming to his grand opening party for Netty's salon, his first renovation, which he had planned himself at considerable expense. Netty had to arrange all the refreshments—Elaine said she didn't know how.

This was how life was, Luther saw. Your fantasies occasionally appeared for you, but only with flaws. You could not possibly encompass every aspect in your dreams. Although he had seen the salon in his mind's eye, equipped and bustling, he had not specifically imagined Elaine right there with him, whole and proud.

He finally convinced her to come to the party, but she did so only in her weakest version. She stood by the new hair dryers all evening, as if she might demonstrate them, refusing even a glass of wine. It was not until he observed her in the harsh fluorescence that Luther saw how much she'd changed since he'd plucked her from her father's house.

"What's the matter with Elaine? She looks so sad," Netty asked after the party thinned out.

"I don't know," Luther said, rubbing his eyes. "I give up."

Even though he had given her cash for a new outfit, she had insisted on wearing a violet formal that he remembered from some point in the past.

"That's too fancy," he said when she tried it on. "Why don't you buy something new?" And although she had taken the money, she had bought a new black purse with it instead, which she now clutched as if she might be robbed.

"I think she wore that dress at homecoming," Netty murmured.

Luther turned sharply. "She did?"

He turned back to his wife with a burning eye. She had been in that dress when he had first been captivated by her, on a movable float, heading somewhere before him. "What year was that anyway?" he asked Netty, who shrugged as Annie appeared at the door, carrying with visible difficulty a pineapple upside-down cake.

Elaine broke her position at the sight of her mother-in-law and moved to open the door.

"Mama will remember," Netty told him.

But Annie said she couldn't remember; she was losing her memory. Years particularly seemed to elude her; she remembered birth and death dates, occasionally when she had acquired a new piece of furniture, but that was nearly all.

"Why do you want to know that for?" she asked when Luther took her coat, completely unnecessary in the summer balm. She had increasingly begun layering herself, as if against a perpetual chill. She wore a sweater even when it was in the seventies, and a scratchy wool one at that.

"Never mind," Luther said and left her to cut her cake for the few people remaining.

After she did that, she walked about the room, touching every object Luther had installed, running her hand over the curve of the washing sink, the faucet neck, the empty cones of the hair dryers. She circled back to Luther, who was standing alone now in the south corner of the emptying room, Elaine exactly opposite. "I want to sit under one of those," she said to him.

"Under what?"

"One of those hair dryers. I never sat under one before."

"You haven't?" Luther was shocked by this fact, and looking at his mother he was suddenly overwhelmed by all he didn't know about the women in his family, the mysteries under their dresses. He'd never thought about what Annie did with her hair. Someone must have cut it occasionally, somewhere, but he realized that he must have assumed that it simply didn't grow.

He'd had too much wine, that was clear. He must have drunk every glass Elaine refused. He looked even more closely at his mother, as if they had just met. She wore a wig, that was it, of course, that same waved black cap, its style never refreshed or changed throughout the years. That's why he'd never thought about her hair.

Luther could barely remember a time when he'd seen her without it, only on the rare occasion when she had been very ill. Then he remembered further that it had been a gift from his father, Horace, that she had told him once, not proudly, that his father had requested that she wear it right after they were married. He'd even bought it—chosen it—for her.

"I'll do better than that," Luther said suddenly. "C'mon. I'm gonna do your hair."

Annie started to protest, a hand to her wig, but he took her by the arm and she relented.

Everyone was gone by now except Elaine and Netty and one of her most recent boyfriends, a man called Booker T something, from out of town. Luther led his mother to a pink swivel chair and helped her into it, turned on a switch and watched with satisfaction as she was elevated to his level with a smile.

"You want me to take it off?" he asked his mother, who continued to smile at him in the mirror.

"No, I'll do it," she said and waited a minute before reaching up and pulling off the cap of black from her head.

And there were the years, there was his old mother, under the disguise she had worn, even with him. Luther had to make an effort to control his face at the sight of her poor skull, black and oiled through grizzled white curls, tiny as at the pubis.

Netty walked up behind them and said, "Mama," with such tenderness that Luther's nose filled with tears.

"Surprised you, didn't I?" Annie asked, her eyes on both of them in the mirror.

"You always surprise us," Luther said.

Elaine had moved from her stationary position and was pulling down the shades on the windows. Luther watched her do this and lock the door and then turn and smile at him, the first smile he had seen on her all night, possibly all year.

"I'm gonna do you up good," Luther said and took a wide-toothed comb, brand-new, from Netty's drawer, and for no practical reason turned on the switch again and raised his mother even higher.

Luther wasn't able to do much with his mother's remaining hair but soap it and dry it and move it around after she came out of the dryer, the curls baked whiter than ever, but she seemed pleased.

"What do you want me to do with this?" he asked, holding up her wig by one strand.

"I didn't realize how bad it was looking," Annie said, reaching for it. She held it in both hands for a few moments, then gave it back to him. "Throw it out."

Luther tossed it into the trash can, but after she left, he retrieved it and put it in the empty supply cabinet instead. It was too intimate for the garbage, and he couldn't stand the thought of its moldering somewhere.

Somehow it was accepted after that evening that Annie was old; she said so plainly now and made requests that Luther had never heard before.

"Change that light bulb for me, honey. I don't want to get up on the ladder." "Run down to the basement and look at the furnace. I can't take those steps."

Of course there were steps to her own room, which she climbed every day, but Luther didn't object. Now that he had managed to leave her house, his mother seemed able to admit how much she needed him. The loss of the wig had liberated something in her, something not altogether bad. She even left off the girdle that she had worn throughout most of Luther's memory, a stained and brutal long-line that hung dripping each night over the bathtub like battle armament. She had twisted and pulled at it for years.

"Take it off," he told her, but she always countered, "I can't; I'm too big."

She was big, but she let him see it now. She was at ease even with her arthritis, which she spoke of openly, rubbing smelly linament on her swollen knees in front of company. And she took Luther's arm when they walked together, now that his arm was needed elsewhere, now that he had a business and a house and dependents of his own.

And she shifted to the third person when speaking of herself, as if she were a character in a play. "Annie's tired now," she said in the middle of a phone call, leaving Luther for the first time to handle the truth of her state.

Netty saw that her mother had given up pretending and was appalled at how well she understood the impulse herself. She went over to Annie's every day now, since Luther was so busy, and withheld from him other reasons for alarm.

For one thing, Annie had begun clearing out her house, gathering together mementoes and knickknacks, which she now called junk.

"I can't stand all this clutter anymore," she told Netty. "Pick the things you want, and the rest I'm gonna dump."

"You'd throw these out?" Netty asked over the

crumbling crafts and souvenirs from other people's vacations, mostly to the South.

"I don't even know where half of this came from!" Annie objected. She picked up a miniature log cabin that said TUPELO in yellow letters on one side. "Who was ever in Tupelo? I sure never was."

"How would I know?" Netty said, annoyed. She didn't want to be responsible for the demise of all this stuff. "You had most of this before I was even born."

"That's what I'm saying," Annie retorted in exasperation. "I've had it long enough!"

She swept off one shelf into a brown paper bag, while Netty stood rooted to the spot. She would have to take it all, she saw, just as Luther had taken the wig, as if it were a relic. They couldn't let their mother discard herself like this.

So she got a rag from the kitchen and dusted each item before placing it in a pile. But as soon as she began doing this, Annie had to make an inspection.

"Oh, that's from your daddy. It can go. This here's from when he went off on some spree. Probably from that Doris."

Netty was much delayed by this running commentary, but dealing with Annie was requiring increasing patience of late.

"Wait a minute, wait a minute," Annie said when Netty tried to toss without her inspection a cracked ceramic bowl. "Loretta gave me that."

Netty was thoroughly annoyed now. "So what? It's cracked. What're you gonna do with it?"

"I'm gonna keep it," Annie said simply. "Lay it over there."

Netty obeyed, but looking at the bowl sitting apart from all the other discards made her mad.

"You're never gonna see that girl again," she said meanly. "If you're not even keeping Daddy's stuff, I don't know why you want a piece of junk from some white girl."

Annie kept her back turned as Netty went on, almost in spite of herself. "Loretta this, Loretta that. You'd think no one else ever had a baby. We all had babies, and I didn't see you moping around about that. I had one and no father to help me, but Loretta, she was special."

Netty's voice had taken on a sneering quality—she could hear it herself. "I got so sick of seeing that pale face every time I walked in this door. And you, running off the mouth, telling her all those stories you never even told me."

"You didn't want to hear them," Annie murmured, not daring to turn around.

"What do you mean I didn't want to hear them?" Netty shouted. "You never asked me whether I wanted to hear them or not. Luther's still mooning around about that shit after all these years, and you're the one that's encouraged it."

She reached for the bowl and saw herself pick it up and throw it on the floor, where it broke into three perfect pieces.

After Netty left, Annie put everything back on the shelves and turned to her closets instead. These were even worse, packed tight with worsted suits and animal hair coats of forgotten ownership. She was distracted from her task by examining the contents of various pockets. She found shopping lists in her old handwriting and faded books of matches which brought fresh pain at the places her husband had gone without her notice, clubs in Cleveland, Detroit—the Cat Club, the Office Lounge, his continual secret life.

She collected $3.85 in change and an assortment of buttons and condoms, losing her resolve in the process. Before she closed the door, she picked up a wooden hanger lying on the floor. ACME FRENCH CLEANERS, ST. LOUIS, MISSOURI, it read. KINDLY RETURN SURPLUS HANGERS TO OUR CANAL STREET LOCATION.

Annie's mother had come from St. Louis, and this relic of her lost family, the old courtesy of those words on a hanger made of a polished wood you never saw anymore, made her lean into the empty coat arms of her past and weep, just as her daughter was at the same moment, out in her car on Sugar Street.

CHAPTER 8

MARCIA MILNER SAT in her backyard, smoking the half pack of Salems she allowed herself each day. She had told Marlon she'd quit, so she only smoked from nine-thirty until eleven, then showered, brushing her teeth and scrubbing her hands so that the smell of tobacco was eradicated by the time he came home for lunch at noon. He had never made an issue of her smoking until Kay; now he said it harmed the girl's lungs.

"But not mine, I guess," Marcia said sarcastically.

"Well, your lungs are your own business," Marlon replied. "You're an adult."

Marcia could not bear this new informal attitude Marlon had taken since Kay had usurped her position as the one in the family who had to be worried about. What was the point of marriage if her husband wasn't paternal, if she couldn't scheme and rail against him, as she once had under her father? Now she was left in the desultory position of mistreating herself all alone.

She'd grown visibly strange, even to herself, since

quitting her job, leaving the whole of the household to Alma, who had also been ordered to smoke in the yard but solemnly vowed not to tattle on Marcia.

"I swear," she said, putting one hand on a tarnished brass cross she wore around her neck, as if such relics held any weight for Marcia.

Increasingly, nothing did. Her fondest thoughts upon awakening were the ten cigarettes, lined up like white soldiers in the secret zipped compartment of her bag, a bag designed with checkbook slots and key ring devices, a bag for the person she had once been, a woman on the go. Now there was no one she cared to see, no destination that was worth taking a shower and confronting her pallid face in the mirror. She only felt anticipation in the morning, when Marlon's Chrysler pulled out of the drive in a fog of exhaust and she had her own cloud of nicotine and caffeine to savor. But increasingly, Kay ruined even this.

"Those things will kill you," she announced when she came upon Marcia in her lawn chair, and Marcia had to keep herself from replying, "Not fast enough."

Kay came outside in the stiff play clothes that Alma had starched and then ironed to perfection. She sat carefully on the ground and looked at whatever came her way; the faces of bugs particularly entranced her, and Marcia had to forbid her from transporting them into the house.

The dolls Marcia had financed sat perfectly ignored on the floor of Kay's closet. The most she would do was pick off their lip color with her fingernails or stick straight pins into their chests.

"So she doesn't like dolls! So what?" Marlon asked her.

"All girls like dolls—she's abnormal," Marcia countered, feeling an expert on this.

"Marcia, I'm not going to tell you again. Stop denigrating that child. She feels it."

But Marcia felt just the opposite—that Kay was denigrating her.

Marcia had been in social work long enough to know that she was in trouble; it was worse when your symptoms had numbers, when you remembered what a cluster of them meant. The only mental health agency in town was her former place of employment, and she would never line up with the rest of the town's misfits for help. But she imagined the scene anyhow, just to savor its painfulness—one of her co-workers decked out in a pantsuit and a dour look of supremacy calling out, "Marcia Milner. Next!"

Oh, they'd have a time with her, if they knew the truth. She'd be drugged and cajoled and encouraged, possibly shocked. All her own old ploys would be unleashed on her—the trick questions and transparent personality tests: *Would you prefer going to a party or being locked in your room?*

Her days of freedom had revealed the shocking truth Alma had always known—you could do whatever you wanted. Why didn't anyone tell you that no alarm went off if you stopped smiling or washing under your arms? Neighbors had begun avoiding Marcia because she had discovered that it was perfectly possible to say to

Marlene Vilgilanti, for example, apropos of nothing, "You're the type of woman who says you were blonde when you were little and used to be able to sit on your hair."

She had the notion that just as she was ready to leave all this, she finally understood it: that everything you came into contact with was important—every fleeting face in a car window, each leafy display had some significance for you alone. She saw that not to live as if this were true—as she had lived, and everyone around her—meant arriving at the big events you were rushing toward hollowly, if at all.

She saw this, but knew it was too late to do anything about it. Her failure had been a large one, since for almost a decade, she'd fixed her gaze on one sole goal: a child. The other things she had experienced but not enjoyed during those early years swished by her mind's eye at night before she went to sleep: vivid Italian meals she had barely tasted, certain moonlit nights when the world of her yard was lit up at her feet, perfect as a stage.

But she had only swallowed these things, then gone back to her room to take her temperature. This was when she was still trying to conceive her own baby and had registered no pleasure at the wrap of Marlon's still ardent arms. She had only thought of his semen, or more particularly that one strong drop that might merge with her. She had grown so accustomed to reducing the world to her fixations that all she had left now was a bitter rue.

If nature had been a model, life—and death, for that matter—would have been easier for her to take. But as it was, she watched the turning of the trees from her living room window as if it were a phenomenon as flat and one-dimensional as a postcard, having nothing to do with her.

People had kept her in the world, but Marcia did not care about anyone now. She had stalled for years over imagining her mother receiving the phone call announcing her suicide. But even this empathy had become worn, like a tattered flag. Marlon's only interaction with her now was corrective. Why didn't she change her clothes and brush her hair? He treated her like an indigent ward of the state whom he was bound to only in punitive ways. He treated Marcia as she had first treated Alma and had then treated Kay.

CHAPTER 9

WHENEVER HIS PHONE rang, Junior Johnson watched it as if observing an unnatural phenomenon. There were whole weeks when he forgot he owned one, surrounded as it was by newspapers and napkins and fried chicken boxes still filled with the gnawed bones of his lunch, his dinner, whichever he remembered to have. One time it had been an upholstery cleaner, asking him what month of the year he usually did his rugs. Junior was so unnerved by this question that he could not think of an honest reply. He hadn't cleaned anything thoroughly since Helene had left.

Later he berated himself for allowing a stranger, a pubescent white one from the sound of her, to make him agonize over the truthfulness of his answer. What did truth matter anyway in such an anonymous situation? It was a measure of how much time he had on his hands that he fumed about such things at all.

Business was bad, that was the main thing. People seemed to die in great waves, and evidently the last surge of them had conspired to do so several months back.

Since then there had only been the freak accidents of children—or so it was claimed; Junior always looked closely at the parents, particularly the father, whenever a dead child or infant was brought in; he looked especially at his hands. This was no time for babies, as far as Junior was concerned, but this did not keep him from fantasizing about his own grandchildren.

He had not been as circumspect about his vow of disowning Elaine as she evidently believed; surely there was some statute of limitations on such an oath, especially one uttered in so much heat and loss. And so for a long while now he had been involved in clandestine drives up and down the alleys near Sugar Street. Alleys were great inventions, Junior thought, perfect for acts of subterfuge, and the only ones that remained intact in Union were on the black—the south—side of town.

Crisscrossing them he caught a glimpse of a blue-coated arm throwing a baseball, brown legs furiously pumping a bike. He saw the back of his grandson's head, perfect as a teardrop; then twin faces—miniatures of Elaine's—as they careened around a corner. It was almost too much, to see them all at once like this.

He circled to find where they were going and was led to the cloying tune of an ice cream truck, a street away. Here he got an even better chance to appraise them, reaching up with their dull nickels. He memorized their jaw lines, their blunt profiles. He couldn't help it; he saw himself all over again.

He made these forays once a month or so throughout

the seasons and deduced from them what he could. He grew adept at idling one street over from Sugar Street, where there was a perfectly accommodating empty lot that allowed him a clear view of their front door. And from there on many twilights he watched the desultory life of the Biggses—of Luther, great arriver and departer, bringing bags of food and taking bags of soiled clothes to the laundromat, wheeling car tires down the sidewalk. A busy bee, this Luther was.

Elaine was rarely to be observed, except occasionally when Junior drove by late at night. Then a woman could be seen—he assumed it was his daughter—moving back and forth in front of a yellow window with hangers in her hands. A few times he saw her conferring with another female deeper in the room, a tall silhouette he thought must be Luther's mother. But the two always seemed to be inside, as if under house arrest.

This vantage point eventually satisfied Junior, who didn't see that he had much choice; it was as if he were looking into another dimension, as separate as heaven, and he did not once think of vacating his car and walking to the door. It would have been like trying to enter a movie set.

In fact, he considered himself invisible; this was one of the side effects of living alone, of working alone, of spending so much time with the dead. So he was astounded at dusk one day when Luther tapped on his car door.

"Hey, Mr. Johnson."

Junior looked at Luther, then at himself in the rearview mirror; he was visible all right. He turned off the heat, then shut off the car, while Luther walked around to the passenger side and got in without invitation.

"I been noticing you around," Luther said simply. "You could come in, you know."

In the dark, Luther's wedding band glinted, a ring his daughter must have placed there herself. Junior's voice was caught at his own exposure; he had never imagined this.

"How is she?" he managed finally.

Luther looked at him, then away. "It's been hard on her. Without her family."

"I thought you all were her family," Junior said, unable to keep the bitterness from his voice.

Luther didn't reply. Both of them looked out at the same winter scene through the windshield. Nothing moved but a lone gray car. Eventually Luther said again, "It's been hard," and opened the door.

Junior watched Luther walk away, across the street, across the spare lawn in front of his house, then through the front door. He could not keep from seeing him as a competitor, and no wonder he'd won. Junior felt like a wizened old man, paled with time, shrunken with silence. He left quickly, afraid that Luther would tell Elaine and that the next person who emerged would be his daughter.

After that evening, whenever the phone rang, he expected something. But a rash of salesmen had evidently traded his number among themselves, considering him a prize.

"Hi, this is Bob from the Chimney Sweep, remember us? We're offering a nineteen ninety-five special."

"I don't remember you, because you were never here," Junior said. "I don't even have a chimney."

An older woman who he first thought was Helene tried to sell him a lot in Florida, a state he loathed without ever having been there. A computerized voice, as frightening as a nightmare, blindly told him about a housepainting special for which he had been randomly chosen.

He phoned Ohio Bell to complain about these calls —crank calls, he called them—but they couldn't help him—no one could help you anymore. And as far as the phone company was concerned, a curt operator informed him, crank calls were obscene ones.

When he wasn't answering the phone, Junior was considering all the postures he could have taken during his encounter with Luther; he could have been sage and grandfatherly; he could have been apologetic for the schism he'd caused. He could have been combative, getting out of the car and rolling around with him in the gravel, something he had actually often imagined. But he had been none of these manly things. He'd been a stunned boy, caught in the act of spying.

Apart from the humiliation of this, Junior hated the waste of time. He saw his life as a film being advanced through a camera, and his had been stuck on some late-middle frame for years. He wanted to speed things up, suddenly; he even felt like opening the camera. Time touched the back of his neck now when he looked in the mirror, not just at his frosted hair, but at something sour and finished in his expression. He looked set in stone.

In this frame of mind, he automatically turned down one of the first pieces of business he'd been offered in weeks, a youngish woman, a wife, a white.

"I can't believe this," the husband said on the phone. "We're over in Sydney, and every funeral home in the area is booked up all week. What do you need? A reservation to die?"

Junior laughed in spite of himself, and this act jarred him. He found himself doing something he couldn't remember doing for years, sympathizing with the feelings of someone white.

"Okay, I'll take care of it," Junior relented. "What is the deceased's name?"

"Milner. Marcia Milner," the man said.

Junior had never done a suicide before, and that was what Marcia Milner was, according to her husband, who met him in the office the next day, his skin the color of eiderdown.

"Can I see the death certificate?" Junior asked and studied the slip of paper under the man's wary eye.

"We're not going to have an autopsy," Marlon said softly. "She's tried this before. Several times."

Junior looked up at this man, whose face was puckered with sadness, as if someone had taken a needle to it.

"This is my first suicide," he said conversationally.

He suddenly wanted talk, even with this aggrieved stranger, who had obviously turned up here as a last resort.

"There's no problem, is there?" the man asked, twisting a wedding band that Junior felt would be removed soon, for good.

"No, no, I just mean that it's always seemed odd to me, someone taking a life."

"Yes, well, my wife—she was extremely unhappy. We kept looking for things to change it." He shrugged. "Nothing helped."

Junior nodded, looking beyond the man's bowed head to his car, parked out front, and the profile of a girl sitting in the front seat, staring straight ahead.

As Junior looked, she swiveled in his direction and presented a burnished, oval head.

"Is that your car?" Junior asked, knowing well it was, having seen the man pull up in it moments before.

Marlon Milner turned without interest. "Yes. Why, can't I park there?"

"No, it's fine."

He followed Junior's gaze. "That's my daughter," he said.

Junior was getting old. The dead weight of Marcia Milner was almost more than he could manage alone. He was so out of practice that when he unfastened the body bag the woman had been brought in, her head lolled out, a tumble of red hair spreading over the table. There was so much of it that Junior was startled; this

was not a young girl after all. But there was not a trace
of revision on her face, no powder, no pencil. He
swabbed it with alcohol and only came up with the slight
yellowish smear of dirt, of life. Junior saw that he had
his work cut out for him. He would have to resort to
all his old tricks to make this woman look peaceful again.

As he worked on Marcia Milner, he imagined the
closets of shoes and jackets she must have left behind.
Junior could barely buy a magazine without thinking
what would happen to it later; he could barely rise out
of a chair without thinking of the long-term futility of
his actions. No wonder he had so little to show for
himself besides this business, which had only flourished
under the optimistic energy of his father. Junior's father
had extrapolated nothing from working in these rooms;
he could have been a taxidermist for his cool working
eye, but Junior had always taken each death to heart.
And this particular one, self-inflicted by a white woman
who had so many benefits, unnerved him. It seemed a
sin to bury so much hair, for example, of a type and
tone that certain relatives of his would give their pay-
checks for. But, of course, it hadn't been enough for
this poor soul, whoever she was. A name, Marcia,
couldn't begin to encompass the lost secrets of these
long white limbs, hairless as glass. We took our mysteries with us, unless we talked enough. Junior's desperate act with Miss Edith, long undetected, had failed
to set him free for more than the moment, and when
he considered what there would be to regret if he died
now, he was filled with a wild impatience.

After he had attended to the body, he vacuumed his rooms and took his first bath in days, almost weeping at the hot water at his ankles. He had deprived himself so long that the least pleasure undid him. Thinking of the white arms folded in his back room like dough, he pressed a shirt, drew back the curtains, and was opening his front door when the phone rang out.

"Daddy," Elaine said, and for a moment Junior lost his place in time, thinking he was supposed to pick her up from school. "Where are you?"

"On Water Street," Elaine answered. "In our new house. We moved."

Junior hadn't driven by the Biggs house since his encounter with Luther. Seasons had changed in the interim, plenty of time for tragedies to occur; he thought of how many people had died since then, for example. He thought of how lucky he was to hear his daughter's voice.

"Let me take it back," he blurted out. "I was a fool to say what I did to you."

"I want to come see you—"

"Come then. Come on. I've got a showing today, but you can drive by later."

"I'm coming now," Elaine said, sounding like Helene, sounding like Junior's mother, now a pile of ashes, fine as aquarium sand.

"Good," Junior said. "Come, then. And bring the kids. I've seen them, you know."

"Luther said."

Junior didn't ask, When did Luther tell you; why did

it take you so long to call? He didn't use one of the old combinations of harsh words from the past. "Bring Luther, too," he said.

Luther came home for lunch that afternoon and found Elaine standing in the doorway with a ham sandwich in her hand.

"You can eat this on the way. We're going over to Daddy's."

Luther looked at his children, standing behind her in their Sunday clothes.

"What's goin' on? Why aren't the kids in school?"

"C'mon, Luther. I've got to do this now." Elaine moved in front of him, sending back in his direction a waft of sweet lemon scent he had never smelled on her before. She had the spare car key in her hand as she walked out the door.

"What's goin' on?" he repeated to Roman, old enough to be his comrade and spy.

The boy shrugged, his mouth full of yellow and pink, mustard and ham. "She says it's an emergency. We've gotta go see our grandpa."

Luther shook his head as his children filed obediently out the door. They had made the move from Annie's, installed carpet and painted ceilings, and now that they were finally settled, Elaine was going back. Luther would have fought her if he thought it would do any good. But he knew the past had its own schedule for displaying itself.

But even knowing this, he couldn't keep from saying

after he got into the passenger side, "I've got to get back to work."

Elaine had already started the car and put it into gear, although she had claimed up until today that she couldn't drive. "Someone else will have to take care of it," she said.

As Luther watched her turn the wheel, he saw her old profile; at some point when he hadn't been paying attention she had turned back into a queen.

CHAPTER 10

ANNIE WOKE UP that morning wanting a Bartlett pear; she couldn't get it out of her mind. It wasn't just the sweet of it she wanted, but the firm flesh under her teeth—her dentures, now. As she lay in bed, the form of it filled her mind, green and gold and speckled, as shapely as a woman. She thought she must be dreaming, but when she rolled over it was still there, and she found that she couldn't move her right side. But both of her eyes still worked and she could see from her bedroom clock that it was nearly noon, although she couldn't work out the day. A beam of sun hit the second hand, which she watched sweep by the twelve with what looked like exuberance, then descend. One, two, three.

She had to have a pear—her right side was incidental to this—and she scooted over until her right arm fell off the bed like an anchor. The phone was down there, black and patient, but her hand dangled over it, a glove. Using her foot, she managed to turn herself over onto her stomach and grab hold of the receiver with her left hand. But then her mind would not tell her either Luther's home number or Netty's at the salon. She managed to dial the zero, and a friendly white woman said, "Mrs. Morris. How can I help you?"

Annie wanted to say, "My daughter has a pink swivel chair in her hair salon that could take me up to the ceiling, if I wanted."

She wanted to say, "Our name is Biggs, from Horace Biggs, dead now, but my name is really Annie Jefferson, from St. Louis, Missouri."

She thought, "I've got five grandchildren, four named Biggs, none named Jefferson, and one named something I don't know."

She wanted to say, "My finches didn't come today, but when I was a girl I had a white goose that laid green eggs. She died and so did Horace and Daddy, and my mother used to cut up Bartlett pears in fours after church in the summertime."

She thought, "Get Luther Biggs for me, born nineteen fifty-two, at eleven-twenty-four at night."

But the copper wire that connected her brain and tongue had been snipped while she slept, and the white woman, so friendly, kept repeating, "Can I help you, can I help you?" until Annie managed, "Twenty-one Sugar Street."

Even from the back of an ambulance, Annie could tell she was being taken to the wrong hospital. She didn't want to go to Good Samaritan; it was Catholic, and since childhood she had been frightened of nuns—their clanking crosses, those bleeding statues—but she could not get the medics to understand that they should take her to Union County instead. The precautions she should have taken now became clear to her in her muteness—she should have written everything down—where she wanted to go to die, how she wanted to be buried, what she wanted to be said. She had tried to broach this topic with Luther once, but he wouldn't hear of it.

"You're gonna outlive me," he said simply and turned his head.

Now he'd have to sort it all out, discover the plot she'd already paid for, not next to Horace, as he surely suspected, but by her parents, back in St. Louis. He would discover this if he looked in the papers she kept in a tin by her bed.

Many times she'd begun to put things in order for this eventuality, but something had always gotten in the way. She thought of her closets, still unsorted, all those dusty figurines still on her shelves, her unswept rugs and unwashed laundry. Luther would have to grow up now, finally, in attending to all this.

These concerns supplanted the image of the pear, but once in the ambulance it returned, transmuted further into a human shape. *Pear* was the only word she could manage before they stuck a needle in her, and the world folded in. But before she disappeared into herself, she saw that even this, her last request, would not be heeded—the medics didn't understand her.

Union had a flame in the sky, the perpetual candle of the oil refinery, and as soon as Loretta saw it, she knew she was home. She tried not to come back here, but she couldn't always avoid it. Her family had insisted on remaining in the region of her past, a certain landscape of streets and trees that was called, as if it could be called anything, Union, Ohio. It was the past to her, but people still moved about in it as if it were potent and fresh. This visit was due to her father's hospitalization for a kidney ailment, but there were always anniversaries and births and funerals; earlier this year she'd come back for Louis's wedding.

Even at twenty-seven, Loretta couldn't imagine growing older, let alone wiser, but these trips made her see that she was doing it anyhow, whether she could imagine it or not. Each time she drove through this town, her face in the rearview mirror was discernibly altered. She only saw it clearly here, on these streets, where she'd once weaved in her car to paint on more eyeliner, where she had idled on the berm to reach inside herself and check the plastic string of her IUD.

Before she'd left on this trip, Loretta had received records she'd requested from the hospital in Cincinnati that were her only proof she'd ever had a child. Away from this town, it was almost possible to believe she'd dreamed that time. But these hospital papers proved it, especially the top left square of the first form, which said, "viable newborn," and then, in someone's hand, the woman's symbol for girl. Loretta had always been certain she'd had a daughter, but this small hieroglyph was the only official evidence she had.

She had scanned the rest of the report with tenderness, as if reading about some anonymous girl in a novel: 17 year old female with hayfever, B positive blood type, 400 cc blood loss.

And then there they were, the physical dimensions of her mystery child: twenty inches, six pounds, eleven ounces, forty weeks, low forceps delivery.

These papers were the first thing she packed for her trip to Union. She folded them lengthwise and placed them in her handbag, where even now, resting on her lap, they caused a certain satisfying weight.

The main street of Union was closed today because of construction, and Loretta was forced to notice her new route, through streets she hadn't traveled in years. Water Street, Milk Street, Sugar Street—the black routes now seemed instructions for a dense, sweet drink. Her own neighborhood commemorated nature, which had been eradicated by the very developments it named—Woodlawn, Hawthorne, Evergreen—the nooks and treed expanses they described were long gone. The downtown streets, on the other hand, were neutral—Robert, James, and Charles—named after generic men. At the intersection of Charles and Milk, the intersection of commerce and ghetto, Loretta stopped at a light and noticed the red sign that had once said LUANNE'S DRESS SHOP. Through those old letters bled the new ones: A BIGGS RENOVATION. She stared at them as if dyslexic. The building was half dark, but she could see the profile of some man inside.

The light turned and she moved on, thinking of

Luther's movements, constrained by these same city blocks during the years since she'd been here, since they'd made their own unnoticed paths over the railroad tracks. If you stayed somewhere long enough, it made sense that you'd eventually have something to show for yourself, a sign announcing your long efforts and occupancy.

She crossed Rob Avenue, and then on Park Street she was slowed by a flurry of movement at Johnson's Funeral Home.

She could not focus on the different centers of activity, just the red ball, dropped by a black boy who moved out into the middle of the street and then froze in front of her grillwork. Then she saw all the faces, not just this boy's, but the head of Elaine Johnson moving down the steps of the funeral home and rushing after him, the same head, perfect as an ornament, that had graced a homecoming float. Then Luther's profile in a car that was parked further south on the left side of the road. Luther didn't see her; he was concentrated on whatever was directly in front of him. But through the glass of the windshield, as she grabbed the shoulder of her child, Elaine Johnson met Loretta's eyes.

Loretta had often dreamed of Elaine walking away with her baby, who had the blond hair and fat cheeks of Loretta as a child. This was the other woman with whom Luther had blended. It was a common thing between them, and Loretta wanted to acknowledge it somehow—to roll down her window, extend her hand. But Elaine's look was intimate without being friendly;

her lips were ready for something, but not necessarily a smile. There was no protocol for a scene like this as far as Loretta knew, and then it was over. A car honked and Loretta glanced back at the trio close behind her in a Ford. She pushed down on the gas and moved forward, allowing through Marlon and Kay Milner and a stout, overdressed woman, whose rouged face was in her hands.

By the time Loretta reached the fourth floor of Good Samaritan Hospital, her father's bed in 424A was empty. It was more shocking to see this than what she had expected: her mild, solid, unflappable father smiling out ruefully, almost guiltily, from his nest of tubes and wires.

Loretta did not think of the most obvious explanation—the truth—that her father had been released already, but the other fact, the one that waited in the wings of the future and would be presented to her eventually, plain as food on a plate, that he was gone, for good. It took her a few moments to gather the courage to ask the nurse where he was, and she breathed in at the luck of her reprieve.

But in the elevator down—the wrong elevator, as it turned out, the one designated for patients—she saw her luck was short-lived. As she moved to the side, two attendants wheeled in a stretcher, and Annie's face, closed as a locket, was pushed into her corner.

"What happened? I know her!" she cried out, dropping her purse.

One of the men jostled the wheels and looked over at her. "Stroke, I think."

Loretta tried to follow them out of the elevator, but they moved behind closed doors that read AUTHORIZED PERSONNEL. Before they swung shut, one of the men turned back and said, "If you want to do something for her, she keeps saying she wants a pear."

Loretta searched everywhere, but there seemed to be no pears in all of Union.

"What do you mean, they're out of season? Don't you think people ever want fruit that isn't grown in Ohio?"

The produce clerk at IGA called the manager when Loretta raised her voice. She almost laughed when she saw him, Darrell Lutes, her teenage suitor and past president of the Audio/Visual Club of Union High, with his little manager badge. "We've got some very nice golden delicious apples, Loretta. They kind of remind you of pears."

She went to Krogers, Big Bear, Ruby's Fruit and Vegetable Stand. She even called home.

"What're you talking about? Your father's waiting for you," her mother said.

She ended up back at IGA, where Darrell Lutes managed to find back in the bowels of the supermarket a single elderly pear.

"You're welcome to it," he said. "No charge."

By the time she made it back to the hospital, Annie had been transferred to Intensive Care.

"Only family are allowed in," the nurse informed her coolly, and Loretta pushed the swinging door with her shoulder and said, "I am."

The nun nurse in Annie's room shook her head to all of Loretta's inquiries. No, no, no, to everything, she signaled; Annie was almost gone. Loretta placed the shrunken fruit in the center of Annie's open palm. Her hand was cool, but her eyes were open. Loretta bent over them and said, "I'm going to find our girl. Hold on."

And then people were trying to summon Luther and Netty, neither of whom were home. The nuns flapped through the room with pieces of paper, stirring up dust motes with their movements.

"Her son is at Johnson's Funeral Home on Park Street," Loretta told a nun as she turned toward the door.

The phone rang out as Junior watched his daughter walk across his room on two feet that he was at least partially responsible for creating and pondered with a sudden slice of gladness all that humans do. They breed daughters and invent telescopes and allocate a single house for the dead, leaving the whole rest for the living—every cracked sidewalk and shadowed corner, all for the living—and he was one and so were his daughter and his wife, whom he knew now he would find. Luther Biggs was just another man, no more or less than he was, whom Elaine had chosen because she knew Junior wouldn't last. But he was here now, his lungs and glands were working now, even in the middle of this chaos, with someone else's dead woman inside.

When Junior was a boy and came upon his father working on a body, he comforted himself by announcing, "This won't happen to us." And because his father never replied, Junior had continued to hope, like a small boy hopes, that death would make an exception with him. It was not until now, at fifty-eight, that he finally faced the facts.

And the phone was ringing in the middle of this, as Elaine shepherded her children to him by the hand. Junior bent and took them to him and Elaine as well, and the phone kept ringing, but he said, "Leave it," for who knew how long such a feeling could be expected to last?

PART THREE

CHAPTER 1

THE SUMMER OF Loretta's pregnancy, Louis had imagined elaborate scenes of his first encounter with his sister, but she had simply walked back into the house one August morning as if she were returning from the Kmart or the dry cleaners—she actually held evidence of both in her hands.

"Hi, Louis," she'd said casually. She hadn't said, "I just gave away a baby"; even worse, she hadn't said, "Look at how you've grown!"

He'd waited all day for some sign of a heartfelt reunion, but his family had walked around with faces blank as plates.

"I know all about your sister," Carolyn said after Loretta had left again two weeks later, this time for college, for good. They'd been standing in a slice of alley between Unity Methodist and Big Bill's Buick, a dank place where, for some reason, boys his age took girls to neck.

Louis had been pondering the entryway to her

dress—a navy triangle without visible openings—and her comment annoyed him; he was sick of thinking about Loretta.

It had taken some time for this to happen—and for everything about Carolyn to cease to be perfection. She had her flaws, Louis saw; it was just a matter of waiting for them to be revealed.

For example, she'd never let him touch her breasts, but encouraged him to rummage around any other area of her anatomy, although the region below her waist was complicated with garter belts and half-slips and, occasionally, a girdle.

"You weigh ninety-five pounds! What're you wearing a girdle for?" Louis had asked the first time he discovered it, and then Carolyn had cried. She cried frequently; that was another thing he hadn't known about her.

But she still possessed that heavy hair and those lips; she still sent him cards at the drop of a hat and professed that she loved him. Louis had thought he would never get over this—those words ushered from deep in her chest into his hair, his neck. He thought it a miracle when he'd first heard them, pressed against the cold stone foundation of Unity Methodist.

But Carolyn used the word so loosely that he became used to it during the years they were together. She also loved devil's food cake and her grandfather and Bobby Vinton and her cat. It was hard to hold on to a holy feeling the way she flung the word around.

So Louis had begun noticing other girls; he saw that this was expected. Even though he and Carolyn had exchanged class rings (he kept hers in his pocket, like a talisman, unless he forgot. It was so little, with its turquoise stone, that there was nothing else he could do with it), he understood this was simply a convention of boys, what you did to assure and comfort during those moments in the alley when you might be viewed as going too far. Louis was aware that the things he was learning weren't particularly admirable, but there you were; he was no longer a boy. He weighed 116 pounds on good days. This was what he wanted, after all.

But his breakup with Carolyn, during their last weeks of high school, had almost sent him back to being a child. He couldn't believe that he was in such a position—the only girl he'd ever wanted, his beloved, railing behind her veil of hair because she'd discovered he'd gone out with someone else. This new girl, Katherine, was no better than Carolyn, was actually worse in many ways. She was a year older than Louis and had already gone steady with five different boys, which meant she wasn't a virgin by any stretch of the imagination. But Louis still found himself saying the unbelievable words, "I don't want to be tied down," when just a few years ago he would have been gladly tied up, bolted down, wrapped around Carolyn forever.

Even his mother had seemed glad when he told her of their breakup. "She was getting too serious," she said.

Her treachery to her own gender astounded Louis: isn't that what girls were supposed to want—for boys to be serious about them?

Who knew? Louis gave up. He was so glad to be

even marginally popular that it sometimes seemed he would do anything to preserve the feeling he had for whole months now—that he finally fit in. He even stooped so low as to describe his breakup to a particularly randy friend of his, Jason.

"She said she was gonna kill herself," he reported to him over a pizza.

"And then I bet she slobbered all over you."

"Yeah—"

"God, I hate it when they do that."

Katherine turned out to be even more of a mistake than Louis had bargained for. She smoked, among other things, and expected Louis to pay for everything and never once sent him a card. In fact, all the girls he had after Carolyn were a decided letdown. He never duplicated that first shimmering surprise of being loved at all.

But he went through girls, like he went through his wardrobe, gladly expanding out of every size. He loved it when his sleeves became too short, when he could no longer button his collar. What did he care? His parents still paid for his wardrobe, along with much else. Now his mother could authentically claim in holiday letters, "You wouldn't know Louis!" He was 5'8", 5'9"; happily, endlessly, he charted himself.

Because Loretta had gone to a college in East Lansing, Michigan, that had over twenty thousand students, Louis had attended the smaller, more conservative and local Mount Ivy, in the middle of a town that only existed for support. He sometimes wondered what his life would have been like without his sister to circumambulate around, but it was no use; he couldn't.

East Lansing, of course, was far more exciting than Mount Ivy, with its cornfield vistas and single pizza shop. The first year Louis was in college a man in Lansing had even set himself on fire to protest the war in Vietnam.

"Did Loretta tell you that?" Louis had asked his mother, who reported this and other tragic news during their weekly phone calls.

"Well, yes, I guess she did," his mother'd replied, and Louis had thought, She would.

On the rare occasion when he and Loretta visited Union at the same time, Louis couldn't keep himself from being impressive. He threw his voice across the yard, announcing baseball scores and fraternity antics (Loretta had spurned sororities, so he'd had no choice). But his sister plainly ignored him, eating macaroni salad from a paper plate next to their grandmother and aunts.

Whenever he brought Katherine there, she defected to this woman's group as soon they arrived.

"Why don't you stick with me?" he asked her.

"Why should I? All you guys talk about is sports." She had a strangely husky voice, from all her smoking, Louis supposed.

But what else was there to talk about? He and his family knew too much about each other; that was the problem. If they started telling the truth, where would they stop?

He was plainly relieved when he had his family to himself. Then they could question him without distraction: What was your grade point again? What was that score? He felt he deserved their attention, which had been diverted so long by his sister.

"You show off so much when we're here," Katherine said as they were leaving one of these dinners, and it was not long after this comment that they broke up for good.

Louis limited his Union visits after that to holiday breaks, when he took a Greyhound accompanied by a great bag of moldering laundry.

"Look at this mess!" his mother said, sorting it into lights and darks, but he imagined that she said this with a certain happy relief, glad that one of her children had finally become normal.

Louis had been dropped when he was a baby—no one ever said by whom, or how; he was just dropped, carelessly as a pan in the kitchen, although surely with a duller thud.

Louis wondered if this drop caused anything about him later. For example, he had no rote memory to speak of, and could only remember facts by association, so his mind was crosswired with words that sounded like something else. To remember Clytemnestra, which he'd once had to do, though he now forgot in what context, he'd had to link her to Clyde's Market on South Street, then to the word *menstruation*. He had to leave it to his dim faculties to smooth off the edges.

Trojan he remembered because of the condoms sold in Harfeld's Pharmacy, which he'd pondered since he was a boy. There was no need to remember the shocking words *lubricated tip*, although some things his brain haplessly stored on its own. Actual Trojans in a blue box had appeared in his family's medicine cabinet at various times in his adolescence before he had reached the blessed stage when he needed to avail himself of them. Whenever he saw them during those years, he wondered if his parents still actually did that to each other, and if so, why they required protection at such a late date. This perplexing period had coincided with Loretta's introduction to the world of sex, and Louis had been vexed by the notion of fertile females all around him; he dreaded the news that his mother, in the midst of her sinus headaches and pot pies, would turn up pregnant on top of everything else.

The way the facts had turned out, he should have given a few to Loretta to take to Luther; he should have asked his father to demonstrate. Carolyn had been left with that humiliating task the first time they'd made love. She had watched him struggle with his flaccid penis for whole minutes, before taking the condom from him and whispering in her cool girl's voice, "I think you have to be hard first."

But what did Louis know about being hard? That was the last thing he'd been taught. He saw how you had to flounder and wound yourself against the rocks —that was the only way you found out anything important, unless you came upon a Carolyn now and then.

By putting her square hand on him she had showed Louis more than he'd ever learned from *The Miracle of Marriage*, a book that had been around his house for ages. But instead of discussing the ovum, chapter 1 should have said simply: find a girl like Carolyn, with strong hands and a tender heart.

By the time Louis realized he'd made a dire mistake in breaking up with Carolyn, it was four years after the fact and almost too late. It *was* too late, if you wanted to consider that she'd had a number of boyfriends during his defection and was no longer authentically his.

He had liked to say "mine" to himself when they made love those first months they were together; he sometimes even murmured it in her ear. This was all he'd ever wanted, he'd thought then, to be on top of someone so fragrant, so open. He felt she loved every hair on his head.

But since their rapprochement, she didn't like him to say that anymore. Being older made you more difficult, Louis saw.

"I am not *yours*," she had said, bolting up at just the wrong instant as far as their lovemaking was concerned. "God, Louis, I haven't even been with you for forty-six months. You've got a lot of nerve!"

"Oh c'mon, I didn't mean it like that," Louis murmured, kissing her neck, the only thing within reaching distance of his tongue. He'd gotten her to lie back down, but it had been all hard work after that. In his absence, her education had obviously included the notion of satisfaction for herself. She tossed him around and twisted her legs and worked them into positions he'd never contemplated before.

"I haven't come yet," she stated in a scholarly voice—she was studying to be a mathematician—when Louis, after painful protraction, was done.

She sat up as much as she could manage and fixed him with a cool schoolmarm's eye.

"Louis, did you hear me? We're not done."

He collapsed onto her like a whale. "Okay. All right. Just give me a minute to catch my breath."

As he worked away on her for the rest of that afternoon, his torso covered with a sheen of sweat, Louis wondered if it hadn't been a mistake to win her all over again. Now that he was graduating, Mount Ivy suddenly lay open in his mind's eye, full of docile, pliant sophomores who would have never caused such a fracas.

But there was something compelling about Carolyn that had remained in a corner of Louis's mind all this time. That first night he'd ever made love to her—or anyone, for that matter—love had been in the room with them, a fat winged cherub, and he'd never gotten over that.

Love wasn't always around now, especially since he and Carolyn had become engaged. There didn't seem room for one more creature, winged or not, in a life filled with so much preparation. How could a wedding—a single exchange of words—require such pomp and circumstance—and so many relatives?

Louis had never known Carolyn had so many—he would have liked to have never known about her Aunt Yvonne, for example, who, mortally wounded by her own brief marriage, attached herself pathetically to any niece or nephew, offering endless—and dated —advice.

"Have you arranged for corsages for your side of the family yet?" she whispered to him at one of Carolyn's family's endless dinners.

"Corsages!" he repeated in dismay.

"I'll take care of it, Aunt Yvonne," Carolyn cut in sagely at his side as she carved a piece of beef.

Louis didn't know how he could endure all this for so long. For some unfathomable reason, Carolyn had insisted that their engagement last over a year.

"But why? Just tell me why, when we could go to the courthouse and have it over with by the end of the week."

"Over with!" Carolyn said. "Louis, this is the biggest event of my whole life, and you're talking like it's a dentist appointment."

"I didn't mean it like that," Louis said—he was often saying this now—and reached for her, but she did a little two-step she'd recently perfected, escaping his arms.

He kept forgetting that underneath the mathematician and competent, demanding lover, a tender young woman still resided. He wondered how many components people could accommodate before they became schizophrenic. How many selves could be integrated into one? Quite a few, Louis thought, observing Carolyn whip out logarithms and manage her orgasm and reach inside a chicken for the secret bag of giblets.

Louis surprised himself by growing wet-eyed when his mother rose out of the pew and placed flowers at the front of the church at the beginning of his wedding. A glance at his father showed he looked weepy too. He had never observed his mother doing anything so public before—seeing her walk up to the altar, as elevated as a stage, was deeply shocking to him.

Carolyn had arranged this, of course; she had arranged all of it in the endless preproduction year. It seemed she had even handled the weather, for the sun shone outside with a theatrical goldenness, even more impressive since it hadn't made a single other appearance all week.

Every detail—and there were hundreds here—the baby's breath, the seed pearls, the coordinated satin bridesmaid pumps—had filtered through her multifaceted mind and most of them through her able hands. Louis could not think of a single thing he had taken care of on his own—even his tuxedo had been rented by Carolyn. She was prudent, after all, and knew he would probably never, at this particular weight and heft, see fit to wear one again.

He watched as her Aunt Yvonne rose also and placed flowers on the other side of the altar—Carolyn's side, presumably. Carolyn's parents were dead, so Yvonne gladly filled the breach in her motheaten blond stole. Louis stole a glance behind him at Loretta, who ac-

knowledged him—and all the rest of it—without averting her gaze.

The exactitudes of Loretta's appearance here were
one thing Carolyn hadn't been able to manage.

"She'll never be a bridesmaid, so you can save your
breath," Louis had said.

"But what about a corsage? Would she agree to dress
in our colors?" (The bridesmaids wore green and pink
and looked to Louis like mints.)

"I don't know!" he had said, exasperated. "Ask her
yourself."

He was already in the junior stage of male abdication
that his father and uncles had perfected. Why do anything when there were these masterful women around?

He wasn't certain now what Carolyn had asked his
sister or when. It was enough of an accomplishment that
she was here in what looked like a new dress, though
obviously not one intended to augment the ceremony.
It was actually red, with a thin trail of white dots around
the collar and hem.

Louis was vastly relieved finally to be getting married. Courting women—courting Carolyn, he adjusted
his thoughts—had been a wonderful effort, but an effort
all the same. Now he had a wife, as he was supposed
to, and he was off the hook at least in one realm. There
were other hooks, certainly—he had to earn a living, at
least half of one, for a while, and soon he would be
called upon to support a household. Carolyn had surprised him by her vehemence in wanting a family. Her
mathematical bent could be oddly diverted; she had the

children arranged already, two boys, two girls, with Louis in the middle of the rectangle.

He still hadn't worked out how he was going to manage this with his generic business degree. He was now vaguely qualified to boss anyone, and at the moment was doing so, on an assistant level, in a taco chain, a position whose long-term possibilities were far from exciting.

But what did he expect—to run the stock market, an international banking firm? He and Carolyn had ended up back in Union, after all.

This was also Carolyn's idea. She had wanted to be near her relatives. She said it was home.

"Where else would we go?" she asked during the early days of their engagement.

"Well, anywhere. We could go anywhere," Louis said to her, without being able to come up with the name of a single other town.

He saw that they were well suited; in a small place, they had turned to each other, and the other possibilities, briefly glimpsed, were blocked by their uncannily equal dimensions. They were both 5'9", and when they hugged, they couldn't see any other horizons.

Carolyn had typed up tailor-made wedding vows on her Smith-Corona, taking out any hard words, like *duty* and *obey*, and replacing them with even more embarrassing ones, such as *cherish* and *adore*, which the old minister from Louis's church read with a distinctive ring of distaste.

Louis said, "I do" gravely, then he and Carolyn kissed and turned to walk down the aisle under the regard of almost every human who was even remotely connected with them. Louis saw them all in a shining instant, as if through great heat—the spectacles of old math teachers and great aunts, the tamed faces of men he had once played football with at the end of his adolescence, when he finally had the girth. He saw men his father sold real estate with, women his mother talked to in the backyard, holding her clothespin bag. Louis thought of the description of dying he'd once read and wondered if that was the next time he would witness such an array of personal acquaintances. It was a great and dizzying moment, rivaled only by his first trumpet solo. How often did people stand and pay attention to you like this?

Carolyn, tripping down the aisle beside him, had transformed herself with froth and lace into a kind of elaborate dessert, the kind he never ordered at the Kingburger, full of sugared air and whipped cream. He wished for a spoon to dig into her; he suddenly wanted to rip off her veil and raise those yards of satin and begin right there on the red carpet of Unity Methodist to celebrate their union in earnest.

But there was the reception line first, where they stood like celebrities, and his sister moving down the conveyer belt of people until she was finally in front of him. She took his hand as she had taken it years ago, saying, "I'm already in trouble, Louis. Can't you see, I already am," and it hit him that if he were twenty-four, then she was twenty-seven and his parents almost fifty, and time skidded around for a moment, like a car on icy pavement, like a dented red Mustang.

Louis never appreciated what it meant to be pregnant until Carolyn found herself so, presumably by him. This was the first time Louis was impressed by his own actuality. When he walked in on her lumbering shape, picking up something off the floor with great difficulty, he thought, in spite of himself, This is because of me.

Of course, it was chiefly because of Carolyn. He was amazed at the ease with which she managed even this, doubling herself in a matter of months, as if a magic dough. She required special attention now, and Louis rushed around like some cartoon husband, soothing her much-easier-to-hurt feelings, tending to her odd distastes and yearnings: she suddenly hated the scent of pizza but developed a passion for beans.

This was what he was meant for, he mused some Saturdays as he sat in front of an NFL game with a beer—his wife banging around their small rented kitchen, which she assured him would soon be too small. Carolyn had a two-story Victorian house in her mind, with blue shutters and pine floors, along with the three other children she planned—and Louis saw she'd probably have them.

Louis had to concede that all he'd had in him was this slightly revised version of the family life he had known twenty years ago in another part of town. This gave him pain only when he thought of Loretta. Con

sidering her made him hope that he and Carolyn continued producing boys. (They already knew about this
one from a test Carolyn had undergone, which Louis
had driven her to, but had been too husbandly squeamish
to watch. And Carolyn had already named, then nick-
named him: Robert, after her father, Buddy for short.)
He hoped these boys would have Carolyn's will and
features; he thought of how he would soothe and comfort them if they were unfortunate enough to inherit his
early ineptness. The future spun out with him under a
basketball hoop, surrounded by a team of his descen-
dants.

Louis had gotten out of taking Lamaze classes with
Carolyn by pleading that he had to work late Wednesday
nights to cover for the unexpected defection of a fry
cook. (He was now manager of his link in the taco
chain.)

A fry cook had quit, but that had been months ago
now, and he'd long been replaced, but the fact that this
had been recently true helped his conscience a little as
he sat bleary-eyed at the restaurant waiting for the hour
he could safely go home.

Carolyn would know—by touching the hood of the
car, the top of the television—if he'd returned earlier.
She was adept at sniffing out deceit, among much else,
and he thought she probably already suspected that he
simply couldn't stomach Lamaze, but didn't want to
admit it. It made him ashamed to think of her with a
surrogate partner—her friend Anna from college—but
at least she hadn't enlisted another man.

He might as well have gone to Lamaze because all he thought about on those Wednesday nights was being pregnant—what it felt like, how it happened. It seemed as astounding to him as dying, yet people talked about it with the same voice that they used for life's other events.

"Joe and I are trying to get pregnant," Anna had reported to him and Carolyn one evening as casually as if they were trying to open a checking account.

And almost every woman he knew had accomplished this miracle of procreation, at least once. Louis now regarded with new reverence the most placid-faced ladies who complained about the lack of salt in the concession island. What they knew! Why weren't they more honored, these mysterious producers of the race? Even their camouflage now seemed remarkable, how they let their powers lurk under banal flip-flops and housecoats. His grandmother, his mother! His sister, who had never once, in all those years, said a peep about those months she'd spent, God knows where, in swollen silence. Once again overdoing it, and now old enough to know it, Louis sat in a sweat those Wednesdays, an exalted, lying husband.

When his mother said, as she often did, "I'm too young to be a grandmother!" Louis had to keep himself from saying, "But you've been one for years." No one ever mentioned Loretta's baby, least of all her.

He'd made Carolyn write to his sister about their pregnancy; he felt nervous about calling her himself.

"Why should I? She's your sister."

"I know that. I just think you should."

He thought Carolyn should do nearly everything involving people. He never knew what gifts to buy at Christmas—he'd never known this—and until they were together he'd gone to the pharmacy the night before a holiday and bought everyone boxes of chocolate-covered nuts, even though he knew for a fact that they were eventually thrown out. Carolyn knew all about this kind of thing—that his mother would like an aqua silk scarf, for example, that aqua suited her coloring. She knew in six months that his father favored a certain style of shirt, a fact Louis hadn't garnered in thirty years.

He sometimes wondered what he did notice on those days he visited his parents, grateful for Carolyn to charm and divert. He sank into his old family house as if into an ancient nest and opened his mouth for his mother's meals like a baby bird.

It was Carolyn who pointed out that Loretta's room had been stripped of any evidence of her and repainted a sexless beige. Louis's was still a boy's blue and was bright with posters that he couldn't believe he'd ever bought. Baseball heroes stared down at him with huge nostrils.

His trumpet case had even been moved into a prominent space in his old bedroom, as if an impromptu concert might at any time commence.

"C'mon, play for me," Carolyn had insisted on their last visit.

"All I can remember is 'The Girl from Ipanema.' "

"So play that."

But he couldn't, even when Carolyn found an old Herb Albert album in a stack of records under the bed. Even playing along with the record, Louis faltered and lost track. Who could concentrate when you had a 160-pound pregnant wife laughing at you in the doorway.

And with each blast of the horn, his boy's life rose up around him; he felt he was tumbling back. He couldn't believe that he'd ever made it out of this room, that the stumbling child he'd once been wasn't still lurking under the bed.

"Don't stop!" Carolyn said. "I was just laughing because you look so sweet."

But Louis rose and ripped the needle off the record, right at the climax, if there was such a thing in a song.

"That's enough," he said, trying out the fatherly voice he would be using shortly.

"Oh c'mon, Louis."

"That's enough, I said," and, remarkably, she heeded him this time.

She heeded him later, too, when he was a father in earnest, when the actual Robert was a visible entity, complicating their world. Louis opened his mouth and out came edicts—"He should be in bed now; he's not warm enough; he's too little to play alone in the yard." Louis couldn't imagine where these words came from. There was an assumption—by both Carolyn and himself—that Louis had garnered information somewhere along the way that now qualified him to be a father.

But where had he learned these things exactly? When

he thought of all the useless classes he had sat through in high school, then college, teachers standing in front of pink maps, he wondered not only where that information had escaped to (where was the capital of Iowa now, the river bordering Bath?) but how his brain had ever produced such fatherly information as how many layers his son should wear or how high it was safe to climb. He thought it simply must be part of his wiring. Louis was sorry that his grandfather had died before he was able to witness this phenomenon.

Louis had to keep himself from quitting his job and following his son everywhere, arms out, as if to catch him in a fall. Since Robert's birth, the world had transformed itself into a place of peril—the wheels of trucks, the edges of tabletops, the heights of windows were highlighted in his mind.

Carolyn was too sanguine about all this, as far as he was concerned.

"He'll be fine," she said the day Robert went off to kindergarten by himself, a day when Louis developed an acute stomach virus and had to stay in bed. "You're the one I'm worried about."

But she didn't know what it was like being a boy, how the world reverted into one great dare.

Granted, Robert had a different style than his father—he threw himself like a fish into the pool the first time they took him; he tromped into his premier snowfall and lightning storm. (Louis remained wary of electricity.)

Louis acted proud of this, but was secretly annoyed. He had soothing words in his throat, ready to dispense, but Robert didn't need them. Instead he won kickball prizes and Little League prizes; he jumped the highest of any boy in Elmwood Elementary.

"A ribbon *again*?" Louis commented dryly when his son walked in with yet another strip of satin. "Is there anything you aren't good at?"

"Not that I know of," Robert replied.

What kind of father would be jealous of his son's accomplishments? Of his excellence in areas where he had failed?

The kind of father he was, evidently.

CHAPTER 2

BY THE TIME he was thirty-seven, Louis wore horn-rimmed glasses that, despite endless adjustments from one of the Harter wives, slipped down on his nose whenever he bent. (The entire Harter dynasty worked in the office; even the children could be seen in back rooms, grinding lenses.) Louis was always bending now, either at work, where he'd been elevated to senior manager (district manager was next, and then the ladder stopped as if at an abyss), or at home, where Carolyn had brought forth two more children, Mia and Heather.

Sometimes she seemed a little confused now, her management askew.

"Maybe we should stop with Heather," she told him one night when they lay in bed as they always did now—in abject exhaustion.

"Whatever you want," he murmured as he slipped into sleep, knowing there was still a shape, four-cornered as a square, fixed in her psyche, and that she probably wouldn't be able to stop until they had one more.

Louis saw that he was dug in deep now; it would take the rest of his energy to see these creatures through childhood and out into the world, and by then it would be time to retire and he and Carolyn would be mere shadows of who they once were. Earlier in bed tonight, she'd talked of the traveling she wanted to do, of how she'd always dreamed of seeing Rome.

"You never told me that before," Louis said.

"Well, you never asked me," she replied, and flipped away from him, like a seal. Her behind had become as fleshy as a pillow, and he put his hand across it. They would never get to Rome; they'd be lucky to make it to Cleveland with all these children, with the way he worked. But Louis didn't say this, partly because Carolyn was already asleep, partly because she already knew.

That night his mother had called after dinner to say that Loretta was coming home for her fortieth birthday, which Louis thought odd. Of all the places she could have gone for such a momentous occasion, Union seemed a poor spot. After all, as a freelance writer, she was the one who had made it to Brussels and Athens—and proved it through airmail letters and postcards.

"Your sister's in Europe again," Carolyn called to him last month when she brought in the mail on top of the laundry, a mound of jockey shorts and bills—how could they owe so much? The postmark was in Greek so Louis couldn't tell where the hell she was.

I'm writing an article on olive oil. Olives really do grow on trees. Also pistachios. Old women like Grandma sit in the shade and crack them with pliers. There's no grass here or lettuce or Thousand Island dressing, but there are a hundred islands. The one named Moni, where I am now, has wild peacocks and fishermen pounding octopus against the rocks.

Last week I met an old woman sweeping the front stoop of a house that hung over the Aegean, encircled by the reddest roses.

"What a beautiful place," I called out (my friend called out—I can't learn Greek).

And she looked at me in surprise and shrugged. "I was born here," she said. Evidently we can't ever see clearly the place where we're from.

But I still see Union—unclearly, then—wherever I go. Certain intersections rise up in my mind, spots where nothing happened, but I see them anyway—the stop signs, the houses on all four corners. I can smell the diesel from the buses.

When we asked this woman if I could use her phone, she took me into her bedroom, as dark and cool as a jewelry box and filled with pictures of the dead and an old black phone that clicked with every digit as I called back home. And in a few seconds, as if by magic, there was Mom's voice. I woke her and Dad because I suddenly wanted them to tell me that everything was all right. I kept asking them this and the reply was so delayed that I thought they were keeping something from me—that Dad was sick or they had decided to disown me after all this time.

Through the shutters of the room I could see the pink stucco walls of the house and a rooster strutting in the yard, and I let her keep repeating, "Everything's fine, Loretta. We're fine," until my heart slowed down and I had to believe it.

It takes a long, slow time for the facts of your life to perk through you, for them to leach down into your soil. Mine are finally settling in me, Louis, and you're all there, embedded in the ground like bright, smooth stones.

Louis hated these letters. For days after, when he sat in rush-hour traffic on Route 287, he was reminded of all he could be doing if he were someone else. Contemplating life at the edge of the Aegean, following a peacock in the sun. What good was it to know this if you couldn't do anything about it?

But these thoughts made him impatient, and it came out in odd ways.

"Aren't you taking lunch now?" his secretary asked

him one noon when everyone—every single tame body—filed out dutifully as sheep.

"No, I'll go later," Louis muttered, though in truth he was starving. And then later at two when his boss found him eating a candy bar on the lawn and remarked, "Is that your lunch?" Louis exploded.

"I don't know! Call it what you want. I'm trying to think a little here, if you don't mind."

"Well, excuse me," his boss said sarcastically. Louis wasn't scared of him; he was as impotent as Louis was.

But, in truth, who could commune with nature in the grassy island of a parking lot? A car was always backing up or pulling in, sending up the exhaust of reality.

Vexed by his narrowness, Louis bought a nature book and vowed to at least expand his children's point of view. But in spite of himself he continued to point out the Big Dipper and robins and maples—the facts they already knew. He tried to get up early to meditate on the meaning of life, but in his office his gaze was pulled to the pile of credit card bills; in his backyard, the cracked foundation of his house. In his own bed, Carolyn's thighs and collapsed cheek lured his thoughts off and away.

Let Loretta live if she wanted to; he didn't have the time.

When his mother called the next week, Louis said, "Loretta's hardly been back since my wedding. What's the big deal now?"

"I don't know," his mother answered. "She says she's got a surprise."

Louis groaned. He hated surprises. "I wonder what that means."

"Maybe she has a new boyfriend," Carolyn offered after he hung up, but Louis gave her a droll look.

"Well, why not? She's only forty. That's not old anymore."

But that wasn't what he meant. Loretta had yet to do a single expected thing in her life, and bringing home a boyfriend for them to meet seemed several decades too late.

Louis had never been able to imagine his sister's life, in New York and the various other cities in which she'd lived. She lived alone, for one thing, which was the first unimaginable element. Louis had never done this, even for a brief interval. He had maneuvered himself from his boy's room to his dorm room and finally to Carolyn's capable embrace. He couldn't have bought sheets or assembled cutlery to save his life.

"She's independent, that's all," his mother said in explanation of her daughter, almost proudly, Louis thought. So was she, it turned out. Whenever Louis started to ask for something at family dinners, his father now gave him a discreet shake of the head that meant he should get up and fetch it for himself. And out of some sort of defiance, his mother had streaked her hair with a plume of white and begun an oddly lucrative career making miniature furniture for dollhouses. On her profits, she visited Loretta in New York several times a year, returning home flushed with Broadway lyrics and corned beef. Amidst the tiny armoires and canopied beds that were now strewn throughout the house, she displayed articles Loretta had written on topics as diverse as income tax deductions and cement. Louis could hear his mother invoking her from the kitchen—Loretta says, Loretta thinks. Miles away, his sister had found her place among them at last.

Louis was now used to this distance, to talking about his sister in the safe third person without having to see her arresting face. He didn't know if he could have done all he had—raised all three children, acquired a Lawn-boy, driven in varying degrees of contentment to work each morning—under her inquiring eye.

Surely she would have questioned the integrity of his sitting every Sunday in the dim Unity Methodist Church, with its monumentally boring sermons—the same ones, in effect, that they'd yawned through as children. Surely she would have asked Carolyn if she were really satisfied with her wrists in bleach half the day.

Loretta's point of view preceded her actual visit by several weeks. Louis sat at night in a cloud of her consciousness trying to defend and comfort himself. But every fact he came upon was accompanied by Loretta's response. I have a house (*and a thirty-five-year mortgage*); I have two cars, a motorcycle, and a snowblower (*but you rarely have time to leave your yard*); I've sired children who will carry on some part of me (*you've had too many; and besides, I had a child myself*).

Louis gave up this line of thought and instead imagined Loretta alone in a narrow bed, covered with their great grandmother's quilts. This is what she had to contend with, at the bottom of it, a bed of her own. He tried to view this as pathetic, but he had actually fantasized for many years about sleeping by himself. Carolyn was a light sleeper who sweated and twisted in her nightgown and insisted on holding on to some limb of his, which subsequently fell asleep. And one child or another usually got in bed with them at some point in the night.

"C'mon, honey," Carolyn encouraged, whatever the reason, whoever it was, so that Louis often woke up bleary-eyed and saw them all as if from an airplane: the bodies of himself and his wife and some open-mouthed child of theirs, splayed out on the mussed sheets as if in a scene from a tragedy.

Carolyn loved this—she would have kept them all in bed with her if their mattress had been big enough. This was her idea of family—a lifeboat of genetics where you huddled together for comfort. This was the last thing Louis's own family had fostered: your bed at least was sacrosanct—you'd never crawl in with someone else.

"It's brotherly love, it's sweet," Carolyn said when Louis went into their children's room one morning and protested that Robert at eleven might be a little old to be sleeping with Mia, their middle one—not just sleeping with her either, but holding on to her rather desperately by the trunk.

Carolyn said this from behind him, blasting him

with her sweet/sour morning breath and Louis had to hold on to the doorjamb for a moment.

"Don't tell me about brotherly love," he felt like saying. "At least I know about that."

Louis had learned that daughters were even worse as far as anxiety was concerned. Not only were the wheels of trucks bigger, but there was also a whole other category to worry over—men.

"Now, girls, don't ever talk to a stranger under any circumstances," Louis counseled.

"How about teachers?" Heather asked.

"They're not strangers."

"But they are when you first meet them."

"I don't mean in school necessarily. I mean out on the street or at the mall or something. And don't ever get into anyone's car."

"What if you're lost in the woods and someone says they'll take you home?" Mia asked.

"When are you ever lost in the woods?" Louis cried out. "Don't get lost, that's all!"

"Louis . . ." Carolyn said in her special delicate voice at the door.

"I'm trying to teach the girls a few things," he said in irritation. She was always horning in.

"You're just scaring them."

"And never take food from anyone. And when you go trick-or-treating, I want to see every piece—"

"Mrs. Morse down the street gave us an apple once, and we ate it," Heather admitted.

"Well, you should've brought it home first. People put razor blades in apples."

"But we saw her pick it from a tree—"

Louis distracted himself for a moment by imagining the sensation of biting into a razor. He shook himself out of it. "The tree could have been sprayed. And that's another thing. People use lawn chemicals, so don't play in anyone else's yard."

"Louis . . ." Carolyn said.

He didn't understand his wife, who had been through enough early tragedies to appreciate the validity of fear. Her parents had died in a plane crash, both of them instantly, or so it was said. Still, on the rare occasion when they had the opportunity to fly, she stepped on the plane easy as you please and even did crosswords during take-offs and landings.

The world was covered with land mines, but could he get his wife to listen?

He'd already begun sizing up the boys in his daughters' classes in a presurvey of who might be a threat. And he turned a wary eye on teachers and principals—it was a well-known fact that perverts lurked in schools.

Carolyn came in and turned off the TV news whenever there was sex-crime coverage—he took it so to heart.

"I don't think we should've had kids—I don't think I can bear worrying about everything that could happen to them," he said one night in bed.

"What made you like this?" she asked him. "You've never even been in a hospital."

"So what! I made it through by the skin of my teeth. And look at Loretta!"

"What about Loretta?"

"Well, look at all she went through."

"I think she might have wanted to go through it. I think you're the one who suffered," Carolyn said.

But it was his daughters' hearts that Louis worried about even more than their bodies. (Robert could take care of his own; it seemed as tough as a nut.) How was Louis ever going to spare them that exquisite torture of having their hearts cleaved in two by an ax?

Years ahead of the fact, he vowed on an open-door policy, where his daughters could bring home any drug addict or sex fiend they wanted. Louis would banter with them and turn up the three-way bulbs, so that his girls could see in this homey light what losers they were.

But that probably wouldn't work either—boys like that were among the cleverest in the world. They could charm his daughters away to the more flattering ambiance of the Unity Methodist alley, or wherever one lured girls now.

If he hadn't had his own past to use as a measuring stick, it wouldn't have been so bad. But even he, the meekest boy in Union, Ohio, had spent at least ten straight years with one diverting thought—how to lay his paw on any available girl.

But what weight did he have anyway, a tired father, compared with the world? Even Carolyn worked against him, buying his daughters Barbie dolls, whose taut tits were their most prominent—and unrealistic—feature, and lately, a sideburned Ken.

One evening he came upon Mia placing Ken directly on top of Barbie in her Dream House bed.

"Barbie and Ken are making a baby," she reported without a trace of embarrassment. "Her name's going to be Suzette."

"Lighten up, Louis," Carolyn said when he reported this incident later that night. "They're going to be fine."

"Oh sure. Mia's obsessed with sex at eight. We're going to have a great time."

Carolyn rolled over. "Just like her father used to be," she said in a soft voice, and he caught a slice of the old face he'd once seen in headlight beams when they'd necked in his car.

"How did we end up with all this?" he moaned, taking her into his arms.

"It's no big deal," Carolyn murmured into his neck. "Everyone does it."

Despite her devotion to her family, Carolyn had begun showing a suspicious interest in Loretta, who had come to represent everything that she, Carolyn, hadn't done. Louis had encouraged her to keep up with her mathematics (a suggestion so suitably vague that it was easy to make), until their third child, when such an injunction seemed superfluous. Keeping track of them all and their clothes and toys seemed mathematics enough.

But lately she had begun saying, "I wonder if I could

have done that," in a wistful way when they saw a successful woman profiled on television. He sometimes came upon her staring out the window, dirty dishes in her foreground, and was frightened that he didn't know what she was thinking. He could not discern her look —was it melancholy, rueful? Was she thinking of theorems, of other men? He doubted it was the latter, but you could never tell. Women remained mysterious to him, even with three in his immediate vicinity. A wife down the street married to an air force man had simply left one morning—left everything, including four teenagers—for good. She hadn't even called them yet, according to neighborhood gossip, and Louis had been more shocked by this than if a murder had occurred.

When Carolyn was out shopping some Saturdays, he roamed their house and thought of how, despite his financing, every inch of it was hers. He had procured the shell, but she had filled in each of the details. There was not a rug or pot or houseplant that hadn't been directly caused by her.

But when he went too low thinking about what she'd given up for him (what had she really given up? She'd had no career when they were married, just the qualifications for one), Louis tried to bolster himself with what he'd forgone as well. But that didn't work either. He would have probably been nothing if he hadn't married Carolyn—just a crusty bachelor living in squalor or an oddball son still with his parents, mowing their lawn for them, buttoning the top button of his Oxford-cloth shirt.

There had never been a dashing, adventurous bone in his body, and he had to concede that Carolyn had saved him, pure and simple, from what he'd lacked. He thought that's what people did—saved each other, sometimes at the last minute—like an inner tube thrown across a lake. That's why people were so desperately coupled; you evidently needed one other person to keep you buoyant, bobbing on the sea of life. But if that theory were true, who had saved his sister?

C H A P T E R 3

ON THE DAY of Loretta's birthday, nine of them were assembled for a picnic—seven family members and two neighborhood children who were Robert's friends. Robert had still not exhibited a drop of Louis's early ineptness—he scanned the horizon for what he wanted, then plucked it. He was his mother's son without hesitation, without a trace of Louis in his face. In his darker moments Louis even wondered if Robert were actually his, if Carolyn hadn't managed one last fling between exits 25 and 34 of Route 75 when she'd returned to Union on her last trip home from college, her diploma wrapped in Saran Wrap. (This made no sense, he knew; Robert had been conceived long after that.)

Louis was in no mood for this gathering; he felt he had been to one too many. It seemed every weekend of his adult life there had been some reason or other to come back here for these family dinners—some child was always having a birthday or it was the anniversary of something. Looking at his mother's covered dishes on the picnic table, he could already taste what was inside them: the baked beans with strips of bacon draped over the top, the anemic macaroni salad—Louis worried that the mayonnaise might go bad in this heat. He would taste his boyhood, a metallic, local taste, in each of these dishes. He knew time had marched on since then—he saw his strained countenance reflected in the patio door, for example—but gatherings like this made him wonder to what end. This all had to do with Loretta, of course.

Suddenly Louis had a strong desire for garlic and vodka and dark gaunt women, as different from Carolyn as he could get. Being here, so prudent, so punctual, had involved a long series of actions he hadn't felt like, had involved changing the oil in the car, changing his clothes, changing his desires. All he had wanted to do today was sit in the sun on the back stoop and look at his grass. He wanted silence—he didn't feel like allowing a single noise to emerge from his mouth. He had even said to Carolyn, "I don't feel up to this. Why don't you and the kids go alone?" knowing he could never get away with it. There was so much he couldn't get away with now.

"But it's for Loretta. You've got to go," Carolyn had replied, predictably, and he had to keep himself from saying, "What has Loretta ever done for us?"

But she had done plenty, now that he thought about it, standing here beside his father as he grilled hamburgers stamped by the Union butcher to a uniform size. She had done plenty, as a bad illness or a natural calamity does, providing a central wound their family had grown around, adjusting, remembering. Along with Carolyn, she had probably kept Louis safe for the only life he could have borne. Such was the force of her glittering, dangerous example that Louis never had to bother finding the thing against which he needed to rebel.

But here at his parents' house on a Sunday in August Louis found himself nervous, as nervous as he'd been on his first date with the woman who stooped in front of him now, wiping snot off their smallest daughter's chin. In his experience, there was usually a good reason for such a feeling. It often presaged some dreadful or monumental event. Certainly, he'd had every reason to be anxious about his first night with Carolyn, since it had ushered in years of such nights, since it had been the introductory session to how he was going to live the rest of his life.

He imagined the possibilities of Loretta's surprise. Carolyn had convinced him that she was bringing home some man, perhaps even a husband. (Loretta wouldn't differentiate in any event, and would have a good practical reason if she had wed. She had privately admitted to him—but not their parents—that once she had actually married an Algerian national, whom she'd promptly divorced after he received his green card in the mail; it was a humanitarian act, she said.) Would she have the nerve to bring someone black home? Did she still even favor such men? What if she were pregnant again? Even at forty, this was possible, though Louis couldn't imagine it very wise.

He paced around the picnic table, then out to the basketball hoop, but Robert trailed after him, and he forfeited the ball—he wanted to be by himself.

"Where the hell is she?" he asked when he wandered back to the table, interrupting a conversation between his mother and wife on cafe curtains—that was the caliber of their talk.

"What's the matter with you, Louis? She's not late. You got us here early," Carolyn said. She clucked in her throat like a hen as a door slammed out front.

"Finally!" Louis exclaimed. What *was* the matter with him?

"Well, go out and meet her, if you're so anxious," Carolyn said, but as soon as she said this, his feet felt mired in cement.

"Go on," she repeated, and it was his mother's voice, telling him to go ahead out the door, up the tree, down the street. He felt a collective hand on his back.

He wheeled away from them and walked up the driveway, past the dryer exhaust where he had sat summer mornings as a child in a gust of fabric softener. The dryer wasn't on now, but the area was permanently tinted with the scent.

He told himself later that he'd known all along. He never had such feelings without a reason, and as he turned the corner to the vista of the front lawn, there it was.

Loretta, at forty, with a head turned grand, was moving around the front of a car as another, younger woman climbed out—climbed out and straightened up, a foot taller than any of them. As he took in this scene, Louis could hear the running steps of his children bearing down on him, could feel them in the very ground. As Loretta moved beside her, the young woman began walking across the lawn. Then she looked up and smiled at Louis, displaying the second brightest mouth he had ever witnessed in his life.

When Louis sat down with his checkbook at the end of the month, he imagined continuing the tradition of holiday letters. He would simply send copies of his family's bills—that would tell the story well enough.

In the last year, Robert had broken three major bones, one of them twice (Louis had decided that he was his, after all); Mia had become nearsighted, seemingly overnight; for some reason Heather had measured her legs and discovered that the left was a quarter-inch shorter than the right, which she had decided made her handicapped and tragic. This was besides the cold and flu and pink-eye epidemics that swept through their house and sent them to Erie Medical, a convenience store kind of doctor's office where you were systematically treated by whatever young, unqualified-looking doctor happened to be freed up while you were in the lobby.

"Why are we all so sickly?" he asked Carolyn, who seemed to have shrunk a few inches herself.

"Oh, we're not. These things are all perfectly normal," she said, but what did she know—she rarely left their house.

And even forgetting his immediate family, his extended one provided plenty to worry about. His mother had hinted delicately of a faulty thyroid and his father had an unspecified blockage.

Louis could relate to that—he often felt blocked himself. It was hard to pinpoint his vague frustrations, but a quick pass by the bathroom mirror revealed plenty: from someone, somewhere, who he'd like to get his hands on, he had inherited a double chin.

At least they had stopped with the three children; Carolyn had become too addled to produce the fourth after all. There had been some complication with her tubes—so complicated that Louis had never gotten it straight—and in the end, to both of their reliefs, she'd had them tied.

Louis could not bear to think of how the two of them had started out, of that spring night when they had walked with sweaty palms to the Kingburger. Had they had been pulled together so sweetly for this—the crush of bills and broken yard appliances and never—ever—enough sleep?

Louis now thought of romance as a lure, a seductive ailment, designed to pull you into the kind of servitude you'd never pick on your own. Sure, his kids made him happy and the heat of his wife comforted him, but couldn't he have used a few more years of playing his trumpet in the spotlight, dunking his basketball in the sun?

But he saw how no one did this if they could help it; people alone were seen as failed and seemed to believe this themselves. You didn't see unmarried women past a certain age riding bicycles, lying in the sun on their lawns (at least you didn't see this in Union). You didn't see bachelors bounding through the world in a free, gallivanting light. Women took them on to reform, to attach to someone.

Of course, there was his sister, but she was in a different category; she was outside of categories as far as he could tell.

"It's Loretta, Loretta, Loretta!" Mia came in singing, her big eyes lost behind the ugliest pair of frames that Harter and Harter had managed to produce so far.

Louis had discouraged her from contacts, remembering his sister.

"They can damage your eyes if you wear them too young," he lied. As a father he lied a lot and had gotten away with most of it, so far.

"And Kay Rita," Heather called out as she ran in.

Louis raised himself from the desk so he could look out the window. Even after all these months he still couldn't get over seeing his sister and her daughter, all six feet of her, pulling up in front of their house. Kay Rita was driving today, and Loretta had her head flung back on the headrest. They looked like—they seemed to be—friends.

The two of them had been back a number of times since that first picnic, which had been indescribable. Louis had feared that his parents might literally die. But they had merely stood up in their sensible shoes and discerned the Dardio face in the young woman before them. In fact, their mother had revealed herself to be a paragon of liberality. "I don't give a damn what people think!" she had exclaimed, unbelievably, as she took her granddaughter in her arms.

Louis hadn't been able to take his eyes off his father, who didn't know what to do with his hands: first, they were ready for a handshake (he was in real estate, after all); then, they went in and out of his pockets; finally, they clenched and unclenched, as if in distress. Then, after his wife hugged Kay Rita, his hands hung at his side until his granddaughter approached and placed one of them against her cheek. It had been almost too much for Louis to witness. He saw that underneath small-town life lurked monumental possibilities, but that the ground sometimes had to shift before they gave way.

He hadn't been able to keep track of the astounding facts that had led to this reunion. Loretta had tried to locate her daughter for years through underground networks and private detectives, but the adoption records had remained stubbornly sealed. She'd had to wait until Kay was eighteen before registering with matching services around the country; then Kay had her own waiting period, until she was twenty-two, before she began searching herself. Loretta reported that their names had been linked by a computer; some artificial intelligence had finally brought the two of them together. Of course, it was just like Loretta not to say a word about any of this until the dramatic final moment, so they could all be threatened with coronaries.

Louis was left in the unenviable position of explaining all this to his children, a particularly painful task with his daughters, in whom he was trying to instill chastity, obviously not a family trait.

He had managed it somehow, talking in sonnetlike terms of blind and early love. Robert had blanched and turned away, old enough to figure it out, but Mia hadn't left him alone.

"But how come Kay Rita's so tall? She's bigger than Loretta."

"Well, her father was tall."

"And she's so tan—and her hair's so kind of—"

"Kinky," Robert finished, looking at Louis with such challenge that he wanted to belt him in the mouth.

Louis had inhaled and looked around for Carolyn, who had obviously vacated the immediate vicinity so this task couldn't be fobbed off on her.

"She's half-black, kids," Louis said. "Her father was—is—black."

There, he'd said it. He could see his children's faces stop; he could hear their brains whirring away. Race had rarely come up with them so far; they lived in a white section of Union and went to a school far whiter than he or Loretta.

"I think Loretta is so brave!" Mia cried out after a minute, giving Louis a stab of fear. That's all he needed—his daughter emulating his sister.

But maybe it wouldn't be so bad after all, he thought now, watching his wife meet his sister and niece at the edge of the lawn. Carolyn was wonderful, but had obvious limitations, as he certainly did, God knows. For example, he worried about how muddled she sometimes seemed, always stuck in the house. Loretta had the sheen of being rubbed by the world at some cost.

Kay Rita had Loretta's face, but she also had Biggs in her; even Louis could see it. For example, she had smartly forfeited the Dardio mouth. Other traits seemed to be blended, as if thrown in a bowl, then rapidly stirred, as he'd seen his grandmother make icing. These were the most interesting to ponder; for example, the shade of her eyes was no one true color but a meld of green and gold.

Louis hadn't spent as much time studying his own children as he spent on his niece, who laughed at him frankly out of her white mouth.

"Louis can't get over me!" she said on their last visit.

"I'm sorry. I must make you nervous."

"It makes me think you love me," she said brazenly, just like Loretta would, and the underside of Louis's face felt irrigated with tears.

Who would believe this? Louis felt it should be documented on video, but neither he nor Carolyn could figure out the video camera they'd put on their MasterCard. And he was so befuddled whenever the two of them were around that he could hardly sit down, let alone operate equipment.

Today was going to be even more of a challenge—Louis didn't know if he'd be able to make it down the stairs. Loretta had asked him if Luther could join them for a family picnic. She still had her nerve.

"Can't you meet somewhere else?" Louis asked, worried about the children again.

"We could, but I want her to feel like she has a family with all of us."

Louis sighed and looked away. "We're not all as big as you are, Loretta."

"Yes, you are. And I'm not big. These are just the facts."

So, okay, he'd said okay. Didn't he always? But he'd strongly suggested that their parents be left out of this particular encounter.

"Fine," Loretta agreed. "I forgot to tell you that Luther's a Muslim now. He doesn't eat pork."

"What does he eat?"

"Well, anything else, I suppose. Is that a problem?"

"No, no."

"No problem," Louis said to himself now, rising, his hands already moist.

This news had rolled off Carolyn's back and sent her into a fit of casserole preparation.

"I've been wanting to try some vegetarian dishes," she said radiantly over her cookbooks. "Let's see, I'll have to multiply everything by four . . ."

His wife seemed to bloom under adversity; Louis thought maybe they all needed a little crisis now and then. He had tried to raise his family, as he had been raised, under the dim light of suburban ease, but he saw that this was not only impossible, but perhaps even unwise.

For example, at the news of Luther's visit, his normally lethargic daughters had begun practicing break-dancing in front of the TV.

"We're gonna dance for him!" Mia reported when he walked into the rec room the other day and found them both twitching in their bathing suits.

"Girls, I don't know . . ."

"We're good!" Heather exclaimed, and indeed she looked as if she were having an authentic epileptic fit.

"Loretta says Luther's a Muslim now, and I don't think—"

"What's Muslim?"

"A religion."

"What do they believe?" Both girls stopped dancing and looked at him; he was always supposed to know.

"Well, they don't believe in pork, for one thing, and I'm not sure about dancing."

"Oh, he'll love it," Carolyn called out as she sailed past in a new braided hairdo that made Louis look twice.

"What'd you do to your hair?"

"French braids," her voice receded. "Kay Rita showed me how."

Louis shut the door of the rec room and stood for a moment in the narrow strip of hall. Kay Rita, at twenty-two, was a hairdresser, an art student, and a masseuse, and was always ready to display these skills on you. She had already placed her golden hands on Louis's neck, giving him such a jolt of release and pleasure that he almost fell out of his chair.

"Poor Uncle Louis, so tense!"

She felt relaxed enough with him to make this intimate gesture, but he'd yet to ask her the thousand questions that roamed around his mind.

How could she waltz so serenely into their white life, without bearing any grudge?

Did she really love her mother, who had given her up, after all?

What did she go as—black or white? Had anyone ever treated her badly?

The thought of this—of Kay Rita's being mistreated in the many ways Louis had seen blacks mistreated both on TV and in life—was hard for him to contemplate.

Loretta surely knew the answers to these and other questions, but he could never really get to her during these gatherings. She sat in a kind of munificence, as if surrounded by a fog. He had never seen his sister—or anyone—look serene before, but this was surely what it was. She regarded him and his family from a tender, slightly elevated distance. For the moment, Kay Rita seemed the answer to all her questions.

"This is my daughter," he heard her say to people who surely already knew. She seemed to like the words. He rarely saw her near a mirror anymore.

"I forgot to tell you that Luther's name is Ahrim now," she told him today when he finally made it down the stairs.

"Ah—what?"

"Ahrim."

"God, what's he turned into? A black separatist or something?"

Loretta laughed—what a sight! He had to keep himself from kissing her.

"I don't know what he is exactly, but he's coming
—in half an hour."

Louis tried to gather himself together as he prepared
the charcoal and to remember what he'd already overheard Loretta tell.

Luther had the same configuration of children Louis
had, was a respectable businessman, and had wept when
Loretta brought their daughter to him the first time.

Louis vividly remembered this detail—that Luther
had sat down in one of his office chairs and put his head
in his hands and cried.

But what else had happened? The other details, if
Loretta had told them, were scattered in his mind with
interest rates and TV plots and his AT&T calling card
number. What were the first words he had said to his
daughter and to Loretta? Did he still love her, after all?

The answer to that was obviously yes, Louis saw,
when Luther arrived. Even after all these years, Luther
still had plenty of love.

Louis had assumed that only Luther was coming,
but then was reminded that with Loretta you could never
tell what might turn up.

Luther was dropped off at the curb by an older man
driving a long hearselike car.

"Who the hell is that?" Louis whispered to Loretta.

"His father-in-law."

"Tell him to join us," Loretta called out, to Louis's
secret distress.

"He'll be back," Luther said as Junior Johnson gave
a nod. "He's going to pick up my wife and kids."

Then he moved to the back door and helped out an old woman dressed in black crepe, who was obviously his mother, Annie. A window opened in Louis's mind, and he remembered what Loretta had told him in the past: that Annie had survived a stroke through the miracle of tubes, first in her nose, then directly into the intimacy of her stomach. A grave had been planned for her, and then a nursing home, but Luther had persevered, sending her to Cleveland, where she was floated in warm fluids and massaged like royalty by attendants.

Finally, she had come back, though obviously not all the way, for she leaned heavily on a cane and her head listed down and to the left. She held it up now for them to look at as if it were a painting, and indeed to Louis it seemed a splendid landscape of a long, true life.

And what a liberal family they were, Louis thought, as they all lined up to greet them, his daughters wearing every piece of jewelry they owned, it seemed to him, and standing stock-still, their breakdancing shocked right out of them. Louis must have done something right.

Luther, dressed in a summer suit and unchanged by the years except for a certain severity around his eyes, shook everyone's hand with a courtly bow, but grabbed Louis by the elbow and pulled him to his chest. Louis blinked in surprise and pleasure, wondering if this were a custom of Muslims.

"I never forgot those papers you gave me," he murmured into Louis's ear. "I knew I'd see you again."

Louis let him pull away after a moment and join Loretta; both of them slipped an arm around the vertical bone of their daughter's back. Then Robert took Annie's arm like some cadet from a movie, and they walked in slow procession to the back.

Louis moved gratefully to the grill in order to steady himself—to his father's spot, *the* father's spot, and not such a bad spot, he decided. The shock of Luther's presence allowed him to notice his own efforts from another perspective—this lawn, for example, a stretch of green that he had seeded, weeded, tended all on his own; the well-formed arms of his children as they swung past with their shining, bell-like heads; the throat of his wife, full as a songbird's. He couldn't help it: he saw happiness there.

He stood grilling meat in a haze of smoky oblivion as his daughters tore in and out of the house, jangling bangles as they ran. On one trip in, Mia turned on her record player and a splash of music fell out onto the lawn.

So his daughters were going to be able to dance as they'd planned. Louis watched Kay Rita initiate the first step, then the glossy heads of his two daughters as they fell in beside her. Luther joined them in a moment, taking off his suit jacket; then Carolyn was pulled in by Mia, laughing as she set down a bowl of potato salad.

"C'mon, Louis," one of them called out.

"No, I can't," he protested. "I've got to watch the fire."

"Louis, c'mon!"

Louis saw the women of his family looking over their shoulders, their heads swiveled exquisitely to the south. Robert was up now, too, the smirk wiped clean off his face, and Loretta was walking around the picnic table, holding out her hand. In the lineaments of her face, Louis saw their parents; everyone was here, after all.

Louis looked at them through the smoke and felt his heart crack—he audibly heard it, like a sheet of the frailest glass. He put down his spatula and threw up his hands and allowed it; he allowed it all over again.